Death in the Forsythia

Death in the Forsythia

A Garden Plot Mystery

A.W. Zanetti

iUniverse, Inc.
New York Bloomington

Death in the Forsythia
A Garden Plot Mystery

Copyright ©2008 by A.W. Zanetti

All rights reserved. No part of this book may be used or reproduced by any means, graphic, electronic, or mechanical, including photocopying, recording, taping or by any information storage retrieval system without the written permission of the publisher except in the case of brief quotations embodied in critical articles and reviews.

This is a work of fiction. All of the characters, names, incidents, organizations, and dialogue in this novel are either the products of the author's imagination or are used fictitiously.

iUniverse books may be ordered through booksellers or by contacting:

iUniverse
1663 Liberty Drive
Bloomington, IN 47403
www.iuniverse.com
1-800-Authors (1-800-288-4677)

Because of the dynamic nature of the Internet, any Web addresses or links contained in this book may have changed since publication and may no longer be valid. The views expressed in this work are solely those of the author and do not necessarily reflect the views of the publisher, and the publisher hereby disclaims any responsibility for them.

ISBN: 978-0-595-52859-2 (pbk)
ISBN: 978-0-595-62913-8 (ebk)

Printed in the United States of America

iUniverse rev. date: 11/11/08

To my spouse, without whose support this book would not have been possible.

Thanks also to everyone who encouraged me to write this, my first, novel.

Prologue

Firefighters were the first to respond to the 11:25 AM call. A three-alarm blaze had broken out at St. Anthony's Girls School on the outskirts of Meadowfield, just outside of Sandalwood.

Sirens wailed in the distance as police cruisers sped to the scene. EMS workers arrived and rapidly set to helping the injured, as students stumbled blindly through the smoke and dust billowing through the open doors and blown-out windows. Frantic administrators hollered above the din to attract the attention of the students, in an effort to gather them all safely in one place where a roll call could be taken to determine whether everyone was accounted for.

Horrified residents gathered in nearby streets, watching the burning building. Already some parents had been contacted by friends and relatives that lived nearby. They rushed anxiously to the chaotic scene.

One by one, students were accounted for and their wounds administered to. Many had gashes to their foreheads and scalps, scrapes from clambering through the rubble, and some had received broken bones.

Hours later, when the flames had subsided, seventy-nine children had been accounted for, and three bodies had been retrieved from beneath the rubble.

A later report revealed that the fire had been caused by a roof collapse, cause unknown, until a further investigation could be carried out.

Chapter 1

▼

He left his house early for the Green Horizons Garden Center, timing his arrival for a few minutes after the doors opened to welcome the day's first patrons. As always, he was anxious to be the first to see the year's new plant introductions. As an avid gardener, he also wanted to start planting as soon as possible. His enthusiasm was partly due to wanting to get out of the house. Being cooped up with his wife over the winter was suffocating, and had put him in a bad mood. Partly it was that he wanted to have the best garden in the neighborhood. He longed for people to envy his landscaping accomplishments.

He was an unattractive man. In his mid-fifties, his pear-like shape reflected his predominantly passive lifestyle, although he tended to lose some of his bulky midsection during the summer months. He had very little hair, just a monk's fringe and a few longer strands that he carefully combed over his shiny scalp every morning and pasted into place. His taste in clothing had failed to stay current. His preference for polyester slacks, and collared shirts, regardless of the day of the week, had the effect of making him look older than he was. Today he wore his customary car coat over his slacks and shirt, as well as a knit navy vest, as it was a chilly day.

As he slid heavily into the driver's seat of his car he was glad that his wife of thirty years had not been able to argue with him about his visit to the garden center. She understood his keen interest in gardening and rarely complained of his outings, however frequent, during the spring, summer and fall seasons. He knew she resented his leaving her without company for hours as he wandered the plant aisles. She had often wondered aloud how he could spend so much time looking for the perfect plant of the perfect height with the perfect blooming period with the perfect color … she considered it an endless, and predominantly meaningless, pursuit.

He had another, related interest. Curiously, it stemmed from his love of gardening. He loved to take photographs. And not just any photographs. He loved to immortalize the thousands of blooms he grew each year. He found that he cherished the subtle color differences between the common daylily and Asiatic lilies, and the various shades of blues and purples of the Serbian and Dalmatian bellflower. He delighted in capturing the most perfect blossoms that graced his garden. Thankfully, sorting and cataloguing his photographs gave him something to occupy his mind and time during the seemingly endless, dull, winter months. He liked order, so he classified his digital photographs by plant species and color.

A separate computer directory housed his precious favorite shots. These consisted not only of macro flower shots, but also of unique and colorful scenes he snapped wherever he drove. A pocket-sized digital camera was his constant companion, permitting him the freedom to take pictures of anything that caught his ever-vigilant eye. He was known to stop on the side of the road to snap a picture of jade and mustard mosses glowing eerily on weather-worn white pines.

Sometimes, he visited parks to take pictures of scenes that took his fancy, an outcrop of brilliant fuchsia rhododendrons in bloom, or a drift of water irises edging a pond. He frowned. He still had to identify what he had captured on those pictures from his park visit a few weeks ago. It had been a cold day, really too early to be out taking photos of emerging spring flowers, but he had spied the scene from the car and could not stop himself from pursuing it. Later, he realized that, in the background of his shots, he had captured two people conversing, a fact that had barely invaded his consciousness at the time, as he had been intent on adjusting the camera's setting to appropriately capture the burgeoning, crimson tulips as they contrasted vividly against a backdrop of white star magnolias blossoms. At home later, looking again at the pictures to see the extent to which the shots had been ruined by the people unexpectedly forming the backdrop, he noted that the parties were unclear. He didn't know why he expected any different. He had intentionally used a fast shutter speed and wide aperture setting to create a clear foreground to contrast with an unfocussed background. He wondered why it nagged him that his attention had been so preoccupied with taking the perfect early spring still shot that he had not paid closer attention to the two parties. He was actually surprised that he had not changed his angle or location to remove the distraction from his shot, as he would normally do. The thought continued to gnaw at him as he drove.

His mind returned to his current undertaking. Why think about pictures when the cold and dreary winter season was over and a whole new crop of new and interesting plants was calling to him?

That reminded him. What *would* he plant in the spot left bare by the rhododendron that died last fall? Some type of deadly, black and sticky, fungus had killed it, although he was diligent to spray his shrubs every spring with an environmentally friendly spray that was designed to protect them from disease and destructive pests. He had lacked the time before the ground froze to replace it. The spot was sunny, with some afternoon shade. There were many plants that would find that a hospitable environment, so that left an almost endless list of possibilities. But the soil was acidic, which was a difficult growing environment for many plants. He could always add more lime to balance the pH level, which would permit greater options.

He mulled over his options as he pulled his faded Buick Skylark into Green Horizons' parking lot near the two gallon pots of ornamental grass that were beginning to poke tender green spikes through the soggy soil. His tires crunched as he left the asphalt and crossed over to an unpaved spot. Preoccupied with his dilemma, he made his way through the aisles to the perennial section. As he looked around, he noticed that not many perennials were available to choose from. *That's okay. I did not expect much selection so early in the spring,* he thought to himself. The selection consisted predominantly of hardy groundcover—leafy ferns, anemones, irises, mosses, periwinkle, thyme and sweet woodruff—many of which were classified as low growing perennials that accepted light foot traffic in shady garden paths. A few other customers were clearly thinking about their landscape and garden plans, and were moving through the aisles, looking at the new plants.

How about another shrub? A burning bush? A 'Korean Spice' viburnum? Maybe a Kousa dogwood or a corkscrew hazel? Each had its own characteristics and features, blood-red bark, or unusual blossoms, making the decision an intriguing one. He looked over to the aisles where the shrubs were kept. It looked like the garden center was already well supplied with shrubbery stock, and he could smell the sweet mingled scent of the rose, citron and cream-colored blossoms in the air. *Great,* he thought. *I'll take a look and see what captures my interest.*

He labored his way to the shrubbery aisles, checking both the common and Latin names of the shrubs as he went. His breathing became labored and he patted his right pocket to check for the presence of his asthma inhaler. Since youth he had suffered from the bronchial ailment, resulting in some avoidance and much caution when it came to physical effort. While it became more problematic during hot and humid weather, he bore the effort that gardening required with stoicism and determination. In most other cases he shrank from physical activity and exertion, to his wife's disappointment.

Vivid yellow forsythia blossoms and shimmering silver pussy willows catkins had burst into bud, drawing his feet nearer. Although he doubted that he would replace his dead rhododendron with such a specimen, he paused to appreciate the yellow blooms and touch the delicate, gray catkins, being careful not to break the wooly orbs from their slim branches.

Suddenly, he became aware of someone standing close to him. He turned to face the newcomer.

"Oh, hi. I did not expect to see you here." He said, a sweat breaking out on his brow.

"Yes," responded the new arrival, steady voice and blank facial expression revealing neither surprise nor expectation to encounter him there.

The plant enthusiast carried on, trying to calm his nerves as his heart galloped furiously, hoping the encounter was coincidental and not intentional. He was uncomfortable with this development. "Take a look at this interesting new forsythia cultivar." Assuming his unexpected companion's interest in the shrubbery, he casually bent down to look at the plastic plant marker and read aloud the name of the budding bundle of branching dark shoots.

As he straightened, a shadow fell across his face. "Oh," he exclaimed as a hand came down on his chest in a forceful, heavy movement. It was the last thing he saw before he died.

Chapter 2

▼

Green Horizons Nursery and Garden Center was a sprawling property of thirty acres on the outskirts of the village of Sandalwood, a small town of about seventy thousand inhabitants. Much of its acreage was devoted to the storage and care of a variety of trees until they sold. Marilee had purchased the center as a going concern eight years ago from an aging German immigrant who had built the business from nothing in the early seventies. He had no heirs willing to take over his legacy and continue the tradition he had established. It was a sad day when he signed over the deed to Marilee, but he could see no other way. He was now in his seventies and had developed such severe rheumatoid arthritis in both hands and legs that he could no longer manage. It was challenging enough when he was able-bodied, but it was no place for someone who could barely hold a pen or walk the aisles of the vast premises without pain. He realized it was time to retire and enjoy his golden years, surrounded by his children and grandchildren, who, for the most part, still lived in the area and remained devoted to each other.

Originally, the size and cost of the property had intimidated Marilee, and she had half a mind to back out of the purchase, but quickly learned that, to be successful in the nursery business, you needed to be able to sell in volume, and you couldn't sell in volume if you couldn't stock an adequate supply of all manner of greenery, including deciduous and coniferous trees and shrubs to meet demand, and that took space. Once she'd decided to go ahead, buying the business had cost her a pretty penny, and she had had to secure a hefty mortgage. In the end, it had been well worth it. It gave Marilee a second career that was invigorating yet was a far cry from the stressful, demanding, rush-rush corporate world.

The property ran on a north-south plane along a major regional road. Coming north, a shopper had ample notice that they had reached their destination, as the tree lot, huge landscaping rockery, guillotine-cut stone slabs and pallets of irregular-shaped flagstones came into view well before the marked entrance loomed to the left of the roadway. And this was a good thing, because many heavy trucks used the road, and the sooner a visitor signaled his or her intentions to turn, the more likely that they would avoid a collision from behind. Marilee always worried about this. One day, if business became sufficiently brisk, or the accidents became more than the occasional fender bender, she would approach the town council to request the installation a flashing yellow caution light warning motorists of turning vehicles.

The nursery purchased most of its deciduous tree stock as 5-year saplings from local specialized growers. At that age, the trees had well-developed root systems, and were hardy enough to be balled and shipped to garden centers around the region. Green Horizons was a primary purchaser. Upon receipt, the fresh saplings were placed in furrowed rows where their root balls were partially covered with soil so that the plants were able to capture irrigated water that was pumped throughout the tree plots. The idea was that the various young trees, such as maple, beech, birch, elm, locust, poplar and walnut would be sold before they were constrained by the burlap that bound their roots. Otherwise, the roots would break free of the burlap and burrow into the neighboring soil. Once a tree became entrenched in the surrounding earth, it became difficult to uproot without causing damage, which was hardly a desirable state of affairs, and could result in the imminent death of the tree if performed without care.

North of the deciduous tree plots were a number of compartments, like roofless, three-sided rooms, each framed by huge concrete blocks to keep the contents separate and distinct from its neighbor. In this section, customers had easy access to bulk landscaping materials, including an assortment of colored mulches, soil mixtures and a selection of gravel aggregates. Marilee had never appreciated the diverse colored mulches. Nowadays, mulch was available in yellow, a deep red, a natural brown, and; could you believe it, black! To her, brown was the preferred shade of mulch. It blended with the surrounding landscape once distributed with care through flowerbeds and under shrub and tree branches. As the natural color of the material, no bleaching or dying process was used. How anyone could consider introducing an unnatural color into the yard was beyond her. Not only was the aesthetic effect jarring, but the environmental aspect was also worth considering. But who was she to say? Her customers' purchases dictated what she stocked, and if they liked the colored mulches then that's what Marilee would sell.

The cubbied area was separated from the patio stones and interlocking pavers by a paved lane to permit customers' vehicles access to the bulk landscaping materials and to provide moving equipment access to the west end of the tree lots and storage areas. The storage area contained a number of Quonset huts in which equipment and supplies were stored to protect them from the elements and from theft. It did not matter where you were, some petty crime existed, and Marilee wanted to minimize the temptation for anyone to steal front-end loaders or backhoes from the premises. These pieces of equipment, along with a rock bucket truck, were needed to move mature trees, landscape rockery and bulk landscape materials in the daily running of the business. They were expensive and well worth protecting. Not only that, Marilee wanted to avoid property damage, or worse yet, unforeseen injury, on her conscience if the thieves turned out to be teenagers who arrived at any cockamamie ideas in a drunken stupor one night.

North of the patio pavers were the covered plant racks. This was where, at the height of the season, masses of annuals in multi-cell packs and fragrant four-celled herb packs were crammed into the available shelves and lavish, colorful baskets hung from overhead beams. In addition, the staff had convinced Marilee to carry a selection of outdoor containers. These containers were made of natural materials such as clay and terra cotta, as well as the newer, fabricated materials that were light and easier to carry, especially once they had been filled with soil and plants. Many customers now preferred these. One could barely tell the difference between a real clay pot and one made from manufactured foam composite. The color and texture was indiscernible.

Marilee knew that a growing trend towards outdoor living spaces was driving homeowners to incorporate all manner of fabric chairs, settees, sofas and loungers into their outdoor kitchen, dining and entertainment areas. She had drawn the line at joining this trend. Firstly, she lacked the space to stock these items, and secondly, she dreaded having to fathom what colors and styles would be popular each year. She thought it was a headache best avoided, and, while a number of her staff had suggested this new product line, she'd delayed making a decision until she saw how her competitors managed with the new concept. It had turned out to be a good decision. Other landscaping centers were finding it difficult to off-load last year's stock in order to make room for new arrivals.

Jutting westward from this area was the indoor display area, where Marilee's and the landscape design office were housed. In the large indoor area between these, ceramic garden art, gazing balls, birdfeeders, birdhouses, tropicals, whimsical stepping stones, self-contained waterfalls, garden tools, gloves and books filled displays of varying heights and configurations. It was the only area on the premises fully protected from the elements, and was where customers and staff alike congregated when a sudden wind or rainstorm made the outdoors temporarily inhospitable. Marilee enjoyed those times. It brought people closer together and it was often how she got to know her customers more intimately, despite the close quarters these situations created.

In a seemingly-endless view north, hardy perennials, colorful shrubs of every shape and size, roses, vines, fruit trees and green, blue and golden evergreens stretched out along organized plots and aisles.

This vast domain was where Marilee spent seven days a week during the planting season, which spanned from early April to late November. Often, she would try to get away at least one day per week; even she deserved some time off during the season. Her winters were spent in a Florida condo on the sunny Gulf of Mexico. While the long summer workdays sometimes seemed interminable, she could always conjure an image of herself lounging comfortably poolside at her condo. The weather was the same, but it was blissful to relax during the long winter months on a white beach with fine sand caressing her tired and calloused feet.

Chapter 3

▼

Marilee Bright savored her coffee as she contemplated the preparation required for the start of the spring planting season. As a successful garden center owner/operator, she knew how much work went into running such an enterprise. It was the first weekend in April, and there were deliveries to schedule and receive, plants of all shapes and sizes to price and place out on shelves, plant markers to prepare, trees, shrubs, perennials and annuals to tend, and inventory stock to monitor and maintain.

She was attractive in an understated way. In her early forties, she was fairly tall for a woman, 5'8", and of medium build. Her blonde hair, blue eyes and welcoming smile usually caused people to warm up to her immediately, which was an important asset in the retail arena where she dealt with employees, suppliers and, of course, the public on a daily basis.

The business was rounded out by a vast array of additional items to ensure a steady stream of her valued customers continued to visit throughout the seasons, including a broad selection of landscape related items, from garden tools, to vegetable and plant seeds, rockery, bulk grass seed, garden art, including iron works and ceramics, and who could forget, whimsical and colorfully painted garden gnomes and sprites, a young child's favorite. In addition, Green Horizons offered tropical indoor plants such as African violets, palm and rubber trees, scheffleras, orchids and philodendrons. The tropicals comprised only a small portion of the business.

This field of work was enjoyable to her. Even as a child she had been drawn to all types of plants, including shrubs, perennials and annuals. She loved how, through her own efforts, she had been able to coax a seed to germinate through careful watering and tending, to the point that it eventually developed into a full-grown plant that she could cherish for years. As a child the free-flowering annuals had been her favorites. At that age, petunias, pansies and impatiens had delighted her. The many large colorful blooms that sprouted from tiny offshoots on each little green plant had enthralling her. Morning glories were a close second. The size of the white, blue, fuchsia or purple blooms that unfurled on each wiry vine was astounding and the papery thinness of the whorl was amazingly delicate to the touch.

As a teen, her parents had let her cultivate a patch of their small backyard, after much convincing. The plot, only about four feet long by six feet wide, had allowed her to try her hand at growing a small selection of vegetables. In her first years she had tried easy, standard crops such as tomatoes, green peppers, parsley and chives, which were great successes. Of all of her eventual pursuits, carrots had been the only failure. To her credit, carrots were well known to be a difficult vegetable to grow, as they required deep, well-loosened soil to permit the root vegetable to grow deep into the earth. Marilee chuckled as she thought back to her carrot crop. The thick stubby two-inch roots were not what you would call a resounding success and were hardly worth cleaning and cooking to add as a side dish to a meal.

Now she enjoyed the variety and challenge that perennials afforded. It was a skilled artist who could best determine how to combine and showcase plantings in the various garden pockets that adorned a property owner's yard. The vast selection of possible perennials that could be planted in a space was endless, and plants could be chosen for color, blooming season, flowering time, height, spread and atmosphere. She thought back to the first time she had gone to the botanical gardens.

Like now, it had been early spring. The amazing drifts of grape hyacinths laced with yellow crocus and patches of brilliant crimson lily-flowered tulips had filled her with wonder and she had never forgotten the sight.

Running a garden and landscaping center was a huge departure from her earlier career. In a previous life, Marilee held the position of human resources director at a number of companies that manufactured and imported anything from kitchen appliances to razor blades. The largest of these, with $10 billion in sales and one thousand employees, had been her most recent employer before she gave it all up, crossed her fingers, and purchased her own enterprise, the Green Horizons Garden Center, eight years ago. Many people fail in attempting such a significant mid-career shift, and she was proud of her accomplishment.

As she looked out the window she noticed that a few spots of snow remained in shady spots between the clumps of budding spring-flowering pussy willows and the still dormant fruit-bearing trees.

She looked happily around her and she heaved a satisfied sigh. Each year the new planting season filled her with excitement. She enjoyed reunions with the local customers as they arrived for their first spring visit full of ideas for new flowerbeds, and meeting new people who had moved into the area, or visitors from nearby towns who had heard of her nursery by word of mouth or through her small ads in local newspaper publications. What could be better than helping people beautify the landscape around them, and surrounding oneself with beauty in the process? Not to mention the company of her competent, friendly and approachable staff.

The spring planting season was off to a good start. Already last week Marilee and Jane Shawson, one of her two long-time right hand helpers, had put out pots of early flowering bulbs and hardy perennials for the early season crowd to place on their balconies and windowsills. Baskets of colorful icicle pansies, mauve grape hyacinth, yellow daffodils, red and pink tulips and purple crocuses brought welcome splashes of color to the store. Slowly the rest of the perennials were making their way to the lots, where customers could wander at their leisure through the ample selection.

Despite the earliness of the season, (Marilee knew that the ground was too damp, if not still frozen, to dig and plant) some die-hard patrons would visit the store, hoping for a first taste of what the season would bring, and select one or two items to take home and protect from the elements until it was safe to plant them in the garden. One of the best things about running a garden center, Marilee thought, was that some gardeners always seemed dissatisfied with the slow emergence of sprouts in early spring, making them anxious for quick greenery and color, and resulting in the inevitable early-season garden center visit. Their concern was usually unjustified. Despite the melting snow and warmer temperatures, many plants remained dormant and were barely starting to feel the first tender awakenings deep in their roots. But to most property owners, the sight of last fall's old, wispy gray hosta flower stems and brown, brittle Black-eyed Susan and Checkerbloom stalks was too bleak. It hardly presented an accurate picture of the bountiful garden that would gradually appear in the months to come. Some foresightful gardeners successfully avoided this sad sight by ensuring that abundant beds of colorful and uplifting early-flowering crocuses, tulips, hyacinths, daffodils, irises, anemones and Glory-of-the-Snow greeted their winter-weary eyes in early spring.

Soon her staff would arrive, looking for instructions for the day. Not that they didn't know what needed to be done. Many of them had been in the business for years and knew their stuff. Even Marilee had become an old hand at the landscape/garden business. It had taken a couple of years to overcome her recurring fear that the business would fail and she would be forced to return to the corporate world. Now in her eighth year, she had come to view those recurring bouts as nothing out of the ordinary and certainly not a concern substantiated by her balance sheet.

As she settled into the well-worn high-backed chair, Marilee reviewed the shipments scheduled to arrive in the coming weeks. While some nursery stock was last year's unsold stock, and yet other plants were grown on the premises, most shrubs, perennials, trees and annuals were received from area nurseries and greenhouses, where mass seed germination and plant cultivation was performed in ideal growing conditions.

Marilee heard a truck door slam heavily. It signaled the arrival of Peter DeHaas, who usually arrived shortly after her. Years in the business had made him an early riser and he was loath to miss a second of daylight. Marilee heard his heavy safety boots clop noisily into the store.

"'Morning!"

"Good morning, Pete."

Marilee's right hand helper, Pete, was the supervisor for the tree farm and heavy lifting work, which included the rockery stone, pavers, bulk topsoil and tree stock. He oversaw a number of trained and qualified people that could be counted on to do a good job.

Born to a Dutch farming family, he was a barrel-chested no-nonsense man that stood over six feet three inches tall. He had a full head of thick white hair and white eyebrows reflecting his sixty-two years. His ruddy completion and large calloused hands resulted from years of physical outdoor work. Despite his tough appearance, he avoided swearing and rough language, for which Marilee was thankful. At the same time, he was a man of few words, and this made it sometimes difficult to determine what he was thinking. Often he made his thoughts known only after careful consideration, and Marilee appreciated his well-thought out, if gruff, commentary, especially when she was faced with a difficult decision on which she wanted his input. He rarely wasted words.

He was a veteran of the business, and had worked at Green Horizons under the previous ownership. The transition had been hard on him (he did not welcome change) and at first he disliked his new boss. It didn't take a sharp observer to see that she knew next to nothing about the landscape and garden business. But Marilee had been patient and eventually he had come to see that she relied on his expertise at every turn, and that he was an even more valuable member of the team than under the previous management. In addition, Marilee had quickly learned the basics, and brought her skills and knowledge up to par by asking hundreds of questions and voraciously reading landscaping and plant books.

Marilee relied on Pete to keep her informed of the required working inventories, which could be a challenge as there was a large market for rockery stone and pavers, and inventory moved quickly. With the boom in residential landscaping, local residents had developed an in-depth knowledge about the various types of stone to add their own flair to their yards. People were also becoming more interested in customizing their terraces and gardens with welcoming areas customized to outdoor living, and slate and flagstones, as well as many types of man-made interlocking pavers, had become very popular as a result.

Marilee deftly poured Pete a fresh coffee and handed the hot mug to him carefully. As she watched him pour milk into the steaming liquid, she asked, "Will you be able to get all of the landscape stone moved to the front lot this morning? We have a lot of trees coming in later this week that I would like to get put into the tree lot before the weekend."

Pete looked up and replied crustily. "Yeah, as long as Tom shows up today. You know, he didn't show up yesterday for his regular shift. If he doesn't show up today, we will be one person short, and we'll be behind in getting the stones in place in order to get to the tree moving."

Marilee considered for a while. "You still have six people, though, right, Pete? Can you make do with four helpers on the lift trucks for the stones, and have two helpers start work in the tree lot? That would help get us in shape for customer needs sooner." The number of employees at Green Horizons varied from as few as ten to as many as thirty-five during the year. In addition to the core team, the majority of the seasonal help consisted of university students looking for summer employment to support their studies. Tom was one of these students.

They both eased themselves into chairs. "Yes," Pete said, "I can have Rob and John work the tree lot together. As we only have five trucks that can do heavy lifting, that will work out well anyway. John can prepare the holes. Rob will use the truck to bring in the trees individually, and John will heel in the trees and mould soil around them to make sure they will be able to get moisture from the sprinkler system. Still, I hope Tom is okay." For a man of few words, this had been a mouthful. Marilee wondered if he was conscious of this fact, and making an effort to more fully express himself. People continue to surprise me, thought Marilee. And it's a good thing, too, or life would be so boring, she concluded.

Jane arrived full of exuberance and spirit, and leaned against the doorjamb. Her lean fingers were wrapped around a mug of steaming coffee. Evidently she had made the all-important caffeine stop in the lunchroom before joining them for a brief morning update.

"'Morning, all. How is everyone? I'm looking forward to getting the rest of the spring-flowering bulbs on display. Sales of spring planters were pretty brisk yesterday, I felt that we might have missed out on sales by not having had enough time to put out some of the new lily-flowered tulips and double-form tulips. You know, the ones that look like peonies."

Jane Shawson was a wiry woman in her early fifties. She was always full of energy, not that Marilee could see where she pulled it from. She was of average height, and maintained a constant page-boy cut to her gray-blonde, thick hair. In Jane's estimation, too much was made of hair styles, and she insisted that it was easier this way. She never had to think what cut the hairstylist should give her; it was always the same. Marilee could vouch for this. Jane's style had remained unchanged the entire time Marilee had known her. Her large blue eyes and open, welcoming smile were a glory to encounter in the mornings, and Marilee had never seen her in a foul mood. The day that happened, Marilee would fall off her chair in shock.

Jane, a qualified landscape technician, had studied at a local university that was renowned for its horticultural, farming and livestock studies programs. Her knowledge was first class when it came to the care and feeding of all things horticultural and Marilee had been lucky to snatch her up when she left her last employer some 5 years before. She was a real gem, and a great help when it came to answering the tough questions that were invariably presented by their always-curious and often ill-informed customers. She loved her job, and it was evident in her interactions.

"We were just getting started." Marilee said. "Sounds like you're ready to get at it, and that you already have your plans all lined up. What are your thoughts for the rest of the day?"

Jane took a moment to contemplate her planned schedule. "Yes, you're right, Marilee. We are all geared up to put out the rest of the hardy perennials, and the early-flowering bulbs, after which I thought we would take a look at the in-coming shipments of perennials. While it is too cool to bring the annuals out of the greenhouse, the perennials will be able to handle the April temperatures. Yesterday I took a quick peek at the new shipments of ground covers and early-bloomers. I can't wait to get them sorted and displayed for our customers. Jaz will water, prune and fertilize the shrubs, at least the ones that can accept pruning and fertilizing at this time of year. And this afternoon, I will ask Karen to water all the perennials."

Karen and Jaz were two of the numerous staff required to receive, inventory, move, price, organize and maintain the huge volume of plant life that flowed through the garden center in an endless river of greenery.

Karen was a relatively new employee. It was her second year at Green Horizons. Like most young people of her age, she was slim, healthy looking and had the smooth skin of youth that was the envy of older people. She had long chestnut hair that she kept in a high ponytail and pulled through her cap. That, together with her summer outfits, made her look like she was on her way to the tennis courts.

Jaz was a married mother of two. She had worked at Green Horizons when her family emigrated from England ten years ago, and, after an unhappy two-year stint as a call center representative, she had joined the Green Horizons family just prior to the time Marilee had taken over ownership of the business. Her husband was a pharmaceutical marketing manager, and her children were in her teens.

"Sounds like you have your staff and your day all organized, Jane. We are opening in an hour, so I will have Justin at the checkout. Let me know if either of you need any help. I'll be here in the office checking on the shipments to ensure that everything arrives as scheduled."

Early in the season they made a point of arriving an hour before the store opened for business. As the season progressed, this practice diminished, as the risk of a killing frost passed, and it became unnecessary to retrieve annuals from the protective cover of the greenhouse.

As they went their separate ways, Marilee returned to her books. *I will keep an eye out for Tom's arrival, if he shows up today,* thought *Marilee.* She could ill afford to employ people who were unable to show up reliably for work.

~

Business was already picking up half an hour after opening. Several customers were lining up at the checkout counter, waiting for Justin to ring in their purchases. The customers chatting cheerfully amongst themselves, each carefully guarding their trolley of treasured perennials, baskets and shrubs.

Marilee strolled by, greeting old friends she hadn't seen since last fall, talking about the weather and learning what had been going on in their lives over the winter months.

When she reached the cash register she stopped to speak briefly with Justin. Over the sound of the snapping register keys she said, "Hi, Justin. Do you need any help?" She noted the growing line-up with concern.

Justin was one of Marilee's more reliable returning college students. His mane of tousled sandy hair hung in his eyes, and he shook it constantly to keep it out of his line of sight. His left ear was studded with a silver ring. Thankfully, Marilee had a policy that banned offensive T-shirts, or Marilee could just about guarantee that he would be the primary offender. He was very conscientious about his job, and was helpful and resourceful. She felt he had a lot to offer and expected that he would do well in his career.

"Hi, Marilee. No, thanks, everything is going well. I can handle it. Gosh, if I can't handle this, what will we do when it really gets busy on the long weekend?" Justin chuckled. "Seriously, though, thanks, I'm fine." He quickened his pace to prove his point.

The May long weekend was known to be the busiest period for garden centers. Officially known to be the area's frost-free date, experienced gardeners had found that the beginning of May was a reliable date and planned their garden activities with that timeframe in mind. The long weekend was also an all-important time for many centers' profitability. Just like Black Friday was a make or break time for retailers, the May long weekend was a crucial time for garden centers.

"Okay then. Ask Jane to relieve you for a break when you're ready, won't you?" She was confident he would ring in the purchases of the four waiting customers quickly.

"Sure thing, Marilee."

As she made her way back to her office, she ran into Trent, one of the three landscape designers on staff.

Trent had joined Marilee a few years ago after finishing landscaping design at horticultural college and a short career with a large industrial/commercial landscaping outfit. He had very quickly found the atmosphere stifling. In his interview with Marilee he explained that the entire process was so profit driven, with little regard for aesthetics that he had to 'get out of there before I lost my mind', as he put it. He disliked the push to slap any tree, bush and ground cover into the design provided it was locally hardy and inexpensive. The focus meant that most landscaping work became a reflection of the previous one, and a blueprint for the next, leaving little room for artistic input and inspired layouts. Marilee had gladly hired him. His ability to grasp customer vision and his creativity in designing delightful and awe-inspiring vistas was now well recognized in the industry. She couldn't possibly see herself creating such lovely yards, and was thrilled when he had joined Green Horizons. Slim, with dark brown hair and a small diamond earring in his left ear, he usually wore a casual look of informal slacks and a golf shirt. His popularity with clients resulted from an air of casualness balanced with a respect for customers and work. In fact, his professionalism and expertise drew clients to him through referrals and word of mouth, a valuable tool in the competitive world of landscape architecture.

"Hi, Marilee," he said breathlessly. "I'm just back from visiting with Mr. and Mrs. James about their landscape design. Have you ever been to their house?" He sounded excited. "They have a great view from their residence on the escarpment! What a lovely property. I'm looking forward to working with them on designing their dream landscape. They want to install landscape stones, a three-tiered deck and some mature cedars and maples to create privacy from their neighbors. It sounds like it will be a great project to design, and hopefully they will ask us to quote on the installation of the project as well. Isn't that great?"

Some lucky residents had been permitted to build or buy existing homes on the raised escarpment, giving them beautiful vistas to enjoy year-round. She was jealous. She could imagine the picturesque setting. The area was sparsely settled due to municipal restrictions, and wildlife—deer, rabbits, foxes and wild turkeys—abounded. She sighed regretfully. Not everyone could have what he wished for.

"It sounds like they have a wonderful property. In addition to the landscape plans you, Stella and Gene have drafted over the winter, I think we may have a full slate for the season. Congratulations, Trent. I always know I can count on you to help keep our design and installation business running at capacity." She smiled at him encouragingly. "What are your plans for the rest of the day?"

Trent laughed. "I'd better get on the design for the James' rear property. They want to get moving on it quickly. They've already decided that they want the work completed by the beginning of August, so it will be a challenge for them to get not only the design finished, the drawings reviewed and any modifications incorporated, landscapers lined up to quote on it, and have all the work completed by that time. The fact is that most landscapers already have a full roster of jobs lined up by February for the coming year. Mr. and Mrs. James are lucky that we're able to quote on the job, only because the Sutherlands decided to cancel their project and move to Seattle, which freed us up to take on one more landscaping job this season."

Design and build projects were managed separately, and not every landscape drawing the garden center created ended up being built by Green Horizons. While the team hoped that clients would want the garden center to build the design, clients could opt to take the drawings to any landscape construction company.

"Sounds like you're really busy, but enjoying it, which is as it should be." She gave him a broad smile. "Speaking of a full slate of things to do, we'll have to start preparing for the regional home show. It's two weeks from now. Will we be ready?" Marilee had assigned him the task of making arrangements for a space and for designing the backdrop for their booth last fall.

He looked at her confidently. "Absolutely. We're all set. And, I've snagged a great location at the show, for which I deserve congratulations, by the way. It will be great." He made as to pat himself on the back all the while grinning.

"Perfect!" exclaimed Marilee. She made a mental note to check everyone's availability for the three-day event. They would have to have at least two, if not three, people at the booth at all times.

Marilee returned to her office. The phone rang. As she picked it up, she heard a blood-curdling scream coming from somewhere outside.

Marilee was so shocked that she put the phone back into its cradle without answering and ran, alarmed, to the front of the store.

Marilee's eyes shot around the area to identify the source of the frightful scream. Alarmed customers and staff were looking in the direction of the outdoor displays, where hardy perennials, shrubs, roses and young evergreens and deciduous trees were housed. "What's wrong? What happened? Is anyone hurt?"

Jaz appeared, pale, frazzled and dazed, holding her hands near her face. "Th … th … there's a dead man in the shrubbery." she said. Jane came running from the perennial aisles. "Jaz," she exclaimed, "Are you all right?"

"I don't know," said Jaz, and dropped her arms to her sides. Everyone saw the red blood staining her gloves.

~

Jane gingerly handed Jaz a cup of cold water. Jaz had calmed down substantially and was now sitting in the lunchroom trying to take in all that had happened. She still looked dazed and confused, as did the rest of the staff that had since gathered. The color returned gradually to her face.

After seeing Jaz's state and the blood on her worn garden gloves, Marilee had gone to see the dead man to determine whether he was truly dead or if First Aid should be provided. None was necessary.

She instructed Jane to place calls to the police and ambulance and post a notice outside before closing the doors to the public. To preserve the scene, Marilee blocked curious staff and customers from entering the crime area.

Now Detective George Blackwell was taking notes and asking questions. He had already been to the scene, and had determined that the death had not been accidental. Thankfully, George was well known by the garden center staff, as George and his gardener wife were frequent visitors to the shop. Everyone knew him by his first name, George, and was thankful that, despite the official nature of his visit, he hadn't insisted that everyone call him "Detective Blackwell", although that would have made his current official role easier.

It was the first time in recent memory that Marilee had seen him in his work clothes. In view of the official purpose of his visit, he wore a gray suit and lightweight dark overcoat, giving him a serious appearance that contrasted sharply with the easy-going jeans and golf shirt clad man she was used to seeing. He was a fit yet solidly built man in his forties with dark brown hair touched with gray where it edged his face. Generally even-tempered in his demeanor, he was periodically prone to frustration and exasperation when resolution of cases proved unduly slow.

"It appears highly unlikely that the victim inflicted this fatal injury on himself. If he did, it would be the strangest death I've ever seen." George said. "The victim appears to have been struck with a three-pronged short-handled garden tool," he explained.

"That sounds like a bed cultivator," intoned Tracey, a long time employee. "It's a tool used to loosen the soil around plants to allow water to reach the roots more effectively. Is that what killed him?"

Everyone gasped in horror. It sounded very brutal, and, until then, everyone had hoped it was an accidental death.

"Looks like it." confirmed George. "But we'll have to wait for the autopsy results before we have confirmation of the cause of death. Until then, we'll have to treat Green Horizons Garden Center as a crime scene, and you'll have to remain closed for business until we've had a chance to complete a full crime scene investigation. Sorry, Marilee."

Everyone was relieved. They needed some time to recover from the shock and were thankful that they would not have to behave cheerfully for customers. That would have been difficult.

"Do we know yet who it is?" asked Trent inquisitively.

In fact, the detective was quite aware of who it was. When he had visited the body earlier to confirm that the man was truly dead, he had taken the opportunity to remove his wallet carefully with a gloved hand in order to check the name on his driver's license.

"I know who it is." volunteered Marilee. "I recognized him when I went to check earlier whether he was dead. He's a frequent customer of ours."

Everyone gasped and shifted their gaze to her. "Oh no!" Jane exclaimed, shocked. "Who is it?"

"It's Stanford Platson."

After the initial sounds of disbelief, everyone fell silent as they digested this latest bit of information. What a sad ending to anyone's life. The staff knew Stanford well, and found the news overwhelming. As she looked around her, Marilee could see people daubing their eyes with tissues as the severity sank in. Marilee herself felt sick, and found a seat to rest her shaking legs. It would not do to collapse in front of her staff. She imagined they looked to her to keep her wits about her and stay strong. She held an unsteady hand to her mouth as her throat choked with sorrow. Someone handed her a tissue, which she accepted absently. Poor Stanford. How could this have happened? We were all here, she thought. How could someone brazenly walk into the garden center and kill a person when they were surrounded by potential witnesses? That would have taken some nerve. Jane, sitting next to her blew her nose noisily. Her eyes were rimmed with red, although she was doing her best to suppress the tears. Marilee put a comforting arm around her, drawing her close, as much to comfort Jane as herself.

"Isn't it possible that he died accidentally?" Justin asked, ignoring George's previous observation. "Couldn't he have fallen on the tool?" Justin looked around him hopefully. "I know, with all the work we have, we don't generally have a chance to get around to working the soil around the thousands of individual potted shrubs and trees, but we do use cultivators in our work. Does anyone know if there was one in the shrub plot earlier today?" Justin looked at Jaz, Jane and Karen. "Anyone?"

While the possibility of accidental death was welcome by everyone in comparison with the alternative, the thought that a carelessly forgotten tool could have caused a patron's death was not a thought the staff relished.

George looked at everyone in the lunchroom. He was as interested as everyone else in the response. "I hope you're not worrying about having left a tool lying around in such a way that someone could have accidentally killed himself with it. It's doubtful that the death was accidental." He stated, shaking his head. "However, it would be helpful to know if one had been in the general vicinity of the crime, like Justin mentioned. Otherwise, we would assume the killer brought it with him, which means that it will warrant closer attention as it may provide additional clues to the killer's identity." George paused expectantly. "So, was there?"

A number of staffers checked their tool belts. Jaz and Karen nodded.

Karen spoke first. "Yes, I'm afraid so," she said disheartened. "I normally keep mine in my tool belt, and it's not here." She checked the pockets again. "I don't know where I left it." Her previous look of grief was now mixed with guilt. She blinked, her eyes scanning the air above her vacantly as she searched her memory. Her shoulders slumped as she said, "I'm sorry." Her frantic mind could not recall where she had last seen it.

Jaz had an explanation. "My tool is in the shrubbery lot, where I was working. I had used it with one or two plants nearby when I stumbled on Stanford." She looked relieved that her tools were accounted for either in her belt or at her current work location. Not that it was much better, since either one of the two could have been used to commit the crime.

"I can't believe someone would use one of our tools to kill someone, and I certainly can't believe someone would kill someone here!" Jane said disbelievingly. "Who would do such a thing?" She paused and thought for a moment. A frightening thought came to her. "You're not considering us all suspects, George, are you?" She bit her lip and threw a horrified glance in George's direction.

"I understand your concerns, Jane. But it's a bit early for me to be making assumptions about guilt and innocence. Standard practice is for everyone to be considered a suspect until they're ruled out. I'm sorry, but I can't exclude anyone on the staff of Green Horizons Garden Center for now. Especially as the crime appears to have been so recently committed. The blood was still fresh and the body still warm. In fact, Detective Jim Peterson has corralled all of the customers that were here at the time, and is currently questioning them regarding what they saw and heard in the minutes before Jaz screamed."

"We will have to interview each of you individually," George continued. "Marilee, can I commandeer the lunchroom? I don't expect it will take all day."

"Of course, George. How do we proceed?"

George turned towards the center of the room to address everyone. "No one is permitted to leave the premises until we've spoken with you. The north plant displays have been marked with police crime tape and are off limits until the body has been removed and the crime scene has been fully investigated, photographed and documented. Please keep to the inside store area until I've had a chance to question you. Then you're free to go home. In the interim, you can call your families, but do not discuss the death, please. It will get out soon enough. Keep in mind, too, that we have yet to advise Stanford Platson's next of kin of his unfortunate passing. Jaz, we'll start with you, since you found the body."

With that the lunchroom emptied as everyone filed out thinking about the unhappy events of the morning.

A few minutes later Trent approached Marilee. "I've spoken with the other landscape designers, and we've determined that we can continue working from our homes," Trent offered. "We have a number of designs in the works that our clients want to see as soon as possible."

"Only if they feel up to it, Trent. It's not necessary. It's been a very trying day, and if people need some time to come to terms with Stanford's death here today, that's okay. The customers can wait. It's not everyday that we are faced with such a crisis. No doubt they'll be understanding when they see it in tomorrow's paper." She placed a gentle hand on his arm. "But thanks for thinking of it. Hopefully George and his colleagues will complete the on-site investigation quickly, so we can be back to normal soon."

"Okay, thanks Marilee," said Trent. If it suited her that they take some days off, who was he to question her? He started making plans for his time off as he moved away, awaiting his turn to be questioned.

Later in the morning, Marilee saw Tom speaking with Pete. *When did Tom arrive?* Marilee wondered. *I'll have to ask Pete when I have a chance.*

~

That night she had difficulty sleeping. The day's horrific events floated like ghosts through her mind. I should have avoided looking at the body, she admonished herself, but wondered if it would have made a difference. Either way, a terrible, brutal crime had taken place, and if she had not seen the body, her mind would undoubtedly have pictured a more gruesome portrait. She rolled onto her stomach and wrapped the pillow over her head, trying to avoid the recurring images. Earlier, she had attempted to immerse herself in a best-selling novel to occupy her mind, before shutting off the light in hopes of falling deeply into an oblivious sleep. It hadn't worked. An hour later she was still tossing and turning.

Eventually, she resorted to brandy, an old insomnia remedy she'd learned from her father. At 1:00 AM she poured herself a two-ounce shot and downed it in one gulp before rinsing the glass and stumbling wearily back to bed.

It had done the trick. Sleep overcame her, but as she slept, frightful thoughts continued to enter her subconscious. Fragmented visions of Stanford lying lifelessly in the shrubbery aisle, his glassy eyes open, his blood drenched overcoat and vest glistening in the sunshine, the deeply imbedded murder weapon protruding at an odd angle from his chest, floated through her mind. Among these horrific images, her mind registered that someone, a mere half-hour before, had handled the grip. Was it still warm, like Stan?

Indiscriminately, people appeared: Jaz's grief-struck face morphed into a evil grin, her hand raised high, menacing her with a bloody cultivator, Tracey's red-rimmed eyes glared at her darkly without a hint of compassion or sorrow. Others, unknown to her, joined the jumble of cruel faces until she awoke in a sweat at 6:15 AM. Relieved that day had arrived, she flung herself out of bed and into the shower in an attempt to wash away yesterday's painful memories.

Chapter 4

The following morning George paid a follow-up visit to Marilee at home.

He pulled up her driveway in his understated dark blue Intrepid, which no doubt helped him keep a low profile, which was preferable in his line of work.

Glimpsing his car as she passed through the hallway, Marilee watched from her doorway as he strolled up. Who would have thought yesterday that her whole life would be changed by 180 degrees within twenty-four hours? One day you're checking your Icelandic poppy order, the next day you're receiving a police detective at your home to discuss a gruesome murder that happened at your business premises.

She had already reviewed the morning's paper, where the murder had been reported in a brief story on page three. Relief flooded her as she noted that her business was not specifically named as the location where the body was found. It would certainly have impacted the garden center's reputation and may have caused shoppers to buy elsewhere. The locals would know anyway, but that could not be helped.

Marilee was curious to see what additional information he had gleaned about the crime. As the owner of the property on which the death occurred, she felt she should be informed of any news, but she knew that the police would not feel the same way and she wanted to be careful not to ask George for more information than he was authorized to share. It was, after all, an open case. Still, she was hopeful he would give her an update.

"Hi, George." She hoped he wouldn't notice as she stifled a yawn.

"I hope you don't mind me barging in like this."

"Not at all. Can I get you a coffee?" offered Marilee. She was on her third of the morning and still waiting for the caffeine to jolt her system to fully awake status.

"Sure. That would be great, thanks. I haven't had one yet this morning, and I feel like I'm running on empty." She took his coat and slipped it over a hanger before placing it into the hall closet as George took off his thick-soled, black leather shoes. She guided him to the kitchen and offered him a seat.

George wasted no time and started with his questions. "Please go over your movements between arriving for work and the time Jaz found Mr. Platson's body. I know we went over this yesterday, but I want to get a clearer picture where everyone was that morning."

"Sure. I arrived shortly before eight o'clock and was in my office most of the morning checking incoming nursery shipments. At various times my staff dropped by to update me on their plans and to discuss staffing issues. At one point I checked with Justin at the cash register to see if he needed help with customer checkouts. I did not leave the indoor store area until I heard Jaz scream and went to confirm what she had said."

"Did you see Stanford Platson when he arrived at the garden center? I'm trying to confirm if anyone saw him, to get a sense of his demeanor at the time of his visit as well as to narrow down the time of death."

"No, I'm afraid I did not, George. Have you asked the others?"

"Yes. Oddly enough, no one saw him enter and head to the shrubbery area. So we have no witnesses able to say whether he was in good spirits or otherwise, or anyone who was able to describe his movements after he arrived. We don't even know if he came alone or with someone else." He shook his head in frustration.

"He could have parked his car and released a herd of elephants, from the amount of visual evidence we have collected. Not a soul seems to have seen him." He passed a hand over his face in disbelief.

"Have you reached any other conclusions?" she asked, pouring two coffees from the boiling kettle and offering him the jug of milk and sugar bowl to prepare his beverage to his liking.

He nodded his thanks. "We have been able to ascertain that he died a short time before Jaz found him, meaning that the perpetrator was in the garden center that morning. Also, we've confirmed that the crime took place at your garden center. That is, he was not killed somewhere else and moved to make it look like he was killed there."

Marilee frowned as George sighed. "You know I'm not in a position to share information about an on-going investigation. But I can tell you that we're looking into all aspects of the crime. And the coroner has confirmed Platson's death as a crime, not an accident, by the way."

He continued. "We will be taking fingerprints from the tool, both from the wooden handle and the metal tines. Because of its grain, wood is generally known for not providing legible fingerprints. However, since the handle has been worn by years of use and weather, I believe we may be able to lift some useable prints, unless the killer wore gloves. We'll have to wait for the fingerprint technicians to let us know. If we do manage to lift any prints, we'll be back to take prints from your staff, both to identify suspects and to eliminate any prints that may not have been left behind by the perpetrator."

He paused to let this new information sink in. Marilee had not considered that there would be additional questioning of her staff. Her naïve perception had been that the disruptions to her staff and business were over and that everyone could move on with their lives without reliving that horrible moment. *I should have known,* she chided herself.

"In the meantime," continued George, "I'm sure you'll be pleased to hear that you're cleared to re-open the garden center. I'm sorry for the inconvenience that was caused, but I'm sure you can understand that, while rare and unusual—thank goodness—crimes or deaths, regardless of where they occur, deserve our full efforts to resolve. Thank you, by the way, for making our work easier by closing your doors and protecting the crime scene immediately upon hearing of Mr. Platson's death.

That was good foresight and helped to reduce disturbance to the area before we had a chance to document it. Unfortunately, no foot prints were obtained from the area as your plant aisles are predominantly strewn with pebbles and mulch."

Marilee was relieved. "Thank you very much, George. I can't tell you how pleased I am to hear that I can re-open Green Horizons. My staff will be happy to hear that we can resume business as usual. When we finish here, I will give them all a call with the good news."

"And Marilee, with respect to the cultivators, you might consider telling your staff to secure them more carefully. While it would not be easy for someone to be accidentally killed by one, a child could easily be hurt. You know how kids are. They find these things and play with them as if they were toys." He regarded her seriously.

"Of course," she replied, jotting a note on a pad she normally used for listing shopping needs. "I certainly would not like anything like that to happen. I will remind my staff to keep them in their tool belts at all times when not in use. They are aware of this rule, but it seems to have slipped some people's mind."

"Perfect, that would do the trick, I think. And this time I'm sure your staff will take it seriously, now that they've learned what can happen when such a tool is used as a weapon." He nodded, satisfied and relieved, knowing that Marilee could be counted on to carry out these precautionary steps.

"By the way, has Mrs. Platson been advised of her husband's passing? How is she? I'm thinking of dropping by to offer my condolences."

George raised an eyebrow. "Yes," he said, "I met with her yesterday afternoon. She seemed quite upset, but I hear she and Stanford have not gotten along in recent years. I'll bet she's relieved he's no longer of this world. I'm always so saddened when I see couples that no longer care for each other as they once did."

He considered for a while before continuing. "I hope you're not planning on snooping around to solve this crime on your own, like the time you investigated the theft of quilting books from the library. This is not a petty crime. The person who did this, man or woman, did not hesitate to kill Stanford. That means we're dealing with a person who does not want to be caught. Someone who has a lot to lose by being found out. That means he or she could easily be driven to kill again if feeling threatened. I say stay far, far away from it, Marilee. The police will handle the investigation."

He sighed as he considered the case facing him. "Not that we have much to work with so far. We have no witnesses, no footprints and, so far, no fingerprints. This case will present a challenge to solve."

~

After George Blackwell left, Marilee headed to the sink to wash the dirty mugs. As she added a dab of foaming dish soap to the damp washcloth, she mulled over the crime, completely ignoring George's admonition not to get involved.

Why would anyone want to murder Stanford Platson? As far as she knew, he was an unassuming person. She found it hard to imagine a reason for anyone to want Stanford dead. Although Blackwell's comments did give one the creeping suspicion that perhaps his wife had gotten tired of him and decided to "knock him off", as they say. Wasn't it easier to divorce him, if they were unhappy in their marriage? There was no reason in this era to remain together if marriage partners were dissatisfied. Everyone knew that almost half of all marriages ended in divorce, and these days barely any stigma was attached to being divorced.

So was there someone else who had a motive, or did Stanford's wife, Glenda, have a more reprehensible motive for wanting him out of the way?

Marilee noticed that she'd been washing the same mug for the last five minutes. *Stop your daydreaming,* she said to herself. *This mug is clearly spotless by now!*

As she placed the mug on the drain board and dried her hands on a soft blue cotton hand towel, she resolved to return to her office, where she had access to the phone numbers required to advise everyone of the return to normal business, and give some thought to what potential motives were at play in Stanford Platson's death.

~

At the garden center, she was the only one there, and things were eerily quiet. While she was often the first to arrive in the morning, she was rarely alone for more than ten minutes, when Pete, Jane or another early arrival made his way to the lunchroom looking for a caffeine fix. Making a brief tour to see whether the police had left the place topsy turvy after searching the premises, she was relieved to observe that they had done a good job of returning items to their original places. Not surprisingly, broken crime tape surrounded the immediate area where Stanford had been found. She shuddered and hastily walked to safety of the office, away from the reminder of the image of death that had burned into her mind.

Marilee settled into her high-backed chair and cleared a spot on her otherwise messy desk. She soon realized that, before doing anything else, she had best call her staff to let them know that they could resume work tomorrow, and call her suppliers to restart deliveries. Everyone she spoke with was greatly relieved that things could return to normal, whatever "normal" was once a murder had been committed on your premises while unsuspecting employees and customers went about their scheduled activities.

She left it to Pete and Jane to call their people, reminding them that they would begin the following day at the usual time and open the doors to the public as normal.

The resident cat, Tabby, padded silently into Marilee's office. Where she had originally come from three years ago, Marilee didn't know, but it didn't matter. The cat had decided to call the garden center "home", and no one seemed bothered by the presence of the shorthaired, marmalade cat. For her part, Marilee adored cats, and Tabby was as friendly as they came. Some people thought she'd been named for the breed, but, in fact, Tabby was short for Tabitha. Jane had suggested the name, and it had stuck, albeit shorted to the more functional "Tabby". It was Jane who cared for her at home during the winter months.

Once Tabby had caught Marilee's eye, she started meowing insistently. *Oh no,* thought Marilee, *during all of yesterday's goings-on, I totally forgot about Tabby. The poor thing hasn't been fed in two days.* She reached down to pet her, and led the ravenous cat into the lunchroom, where Marilee opened a can of cat food, mixed in some dry food and provided fresh water. Not surprisingly, the cat ignored Marilee entirely as she set to greedily gobbling up the meaty morsels.

Having seen to the feline's hunger, Marilee headed back to her office to continue where she left off, calling suppliers about deliveries and leaving messages for the ones she could not reach in person.

It wasn't long before Tabby was back, no doubt looking for some company this time. The cat leapt effortlessly onto Marilee's disorganized desk and made herself comfortable beside a stone penholder Marilee had received at a recent landscaping conference. The cat didn't seem to be bothered by the mountains of papers covering the surface in semi-organized piles that only Marilee understood.

Marilee patted Tabby, who purred contentedly, her tail gracefully flicking the papers as Marilee was finally ready to begin the task that really intrigued her. She retrieved a well-worn pad from her desk drawer and flipped to a clean page. She wrote "motives" across the top in her usual scrawl. It seemed a strange approach, she realized. Normally, in criminal investigations, one usually started with suspects, not motives. However, she knew next to nothing about Stanford Platson. What little she knew of him could fit on a tiny cue card. So what did she know? He was married. As an avid gardener, he was a frequent visitor to the garden center. He was an active participant in the annual garden tour, offering his property as one of the numerous tour stops each year.

In the meantime, the cat had combed her whiskers with her paws to locate any remaining food particles that may have escaped her attention. Marilee picked her up and placed the amenable cat on her lap as she leaned back in her chair. Tabby reveled in the attention while Marilee absently petted her fur and scratched her chin.

Marilee realized that she didn't know Stanford Platson very well, certainly not beyond the obvious. She did not even know what he did for a living. Did he have a lucrative career? Marilee didn't think so based on the faded old Buick Skylark he had driven for as long as Marilee could remember. Did he have disgruntled business partners? She chastised herself for not knowing more. *That's it,* she told herself, *you should get to know your clientele better.*

And with that thought she resolved to visit Glenda Platson to offer her condolences and learn more about her deceased husband.

She glanced at the almost-blank page in front of her and realized she'd written not one additional word since having written the heading at the top of the page. To make the exercise worthwhile, she wrote "substantial life insurance payout?" on the lined paper. *There,* she thought to herself, *that's one possible motive.* And she closed the pad and returned it to her upper right desk drawer for another time. The cat, disturbed by this sudden noise and activity, leapt from Marilee's lap to find a quieter, more peaceful resting place elsewhere on the premises.

Chapter 5

▼

The following day, things were back to normal at Green Horizons. Early in the morning, Pete and Jane arrived and dropped by Marilee's office to find out if she had learned anything new about the death of Stanford Platson. They were clearly curious whether anything new had developed in the preceding forty-eight hours.

Marilee updated them with the latest news.

"You could find out who killed him, Marilee," an excited Jane said. "You've always been interested in solving mysteries, and look how successful you were at solving that spate of book thefts from the library. You have a great sense of curiosity and are really good at recognizing facts that are important to the case."

"Murder is not quite on the same scale as book thefts," Marilee pointed out. "It's a much more complex crime, with serious personal risks."

"Are you seriously considering trying to solve this murder?" asked Pete incredulously. "I don't think it's a good idea, but I know you'll do whatever you set your mind to doing."

Marilee looked up. At least she knew now how her two right hand people felt about her inclinations. "We'll see," said Marilee noncommittally.

Secretly, there was no doubt in her mind that she was going to try to find out who had murdered the unfortunate Stanford Platson. Was there a better reason than that the crime took place on the garden center's own premises during business hours?

"I'm glad it wasn't Jaz that was killed. Imagine, she was in the exact location that Mr. Platson was standing, just a few minutes after he was killed!" exclaimed Jane.

"Yes, that's a frightful thought," responded Marilee furrowing her brow, "but I don't think it would have been Jaz. It seems to me that Mr. Platson was intentionally targeted. I don't think the killer was planning to kill just anyone."

Pete agreed, nodding. "I have to say I agree with Marilee, Jane." He could not explain why, but that was his impression.

Jane appeared unconvinced but said nothing.

"That reminds me, Pete. I've been meaning to ask you," asked Marilee, "I saw that Tom made it to work eventually, on Monday. What did he give as his reason for being late, Pete?"

"He said his car had a flat on the way to work, and it took him over an hour to loosen the lug nuts on the wheel so he could replace the flat tire with a spare. He seemed sincerely apologetic, so I let him off with a warning, and told him to keep his car well maintained, so that these types of things don't prevent him from being at work on time," Pete said. "He's a good enough worker when he's here and a pretty nice guy, so I didn't want to be too hard on him." He added.

Marilee did not bother to comment on the suitability of his handling of the situation with Tom. He was much too senior to require her praise or reinforcement. "I see," she said simply, and decided that it wasn't worth pursuing for the moment. "Changing subjects, what do the two of you know about Stanford Platson? It seems so curious that someone would kill him in such a public place and in such a forceful way. It would have taken a person with a strong motive and nerves of steel to feel they wouldn't be caught red-handed." She shook her head.

"Sounds to me like you *are* planning to investigate," Jane was quick to observe, with a mischievous glint in her eye. "I think you should do it. Wouldn't it be great if you were the one to solve this crime?"

Marilee was embarrassed that her question had been so transparent. She couldn't fault Jane, though; she was right. "I realized I don't know very much about him," she replied noncommittally as she shrugged her shoulders. "I thought it might be an opportunity to learn more about who he was. He was, after all, killed at Green Horizons."

The look on Jane's face indicated she thought that was a weak reason, but she let it pass. Anyway, this gave her an opportunity to gossip a bit, which she was not averse to doing, on occasion. "I have heard rumors that the Platsons were not happy at home." Jane responded. "Remember, they used to come to the garden center together, but when was the last time you saw her here?" *Good point,* thought Marilee. She and Pete nodded their agreement.

"He is also obviously a keen gardener, based on his frequent visits here." Jane continued. "I hear that he is a financial controller at Sturdy Roofing Installations on Wilson Street in town. From what I've heard, he worked there for years. He was chief accountant until two years ago, when the existing controller left, and Stanford was promoted to take her place."

"I've seen him in town a few times," added Pete, flipping his cap off his head and scratching his scalp through his thick white hair. "He pretty much keeps to himself, doesn't say much, even when you talk to him directly. I ran into him a few weeks ago at the Buy and Save, and he didn't say much more than 'hello'." Peter continued. He glanced alternately at his boss and his colleague as he worked on recalling anything else he knew about Stanford. "Over the years he's placed some orders for delivery of truckloads of triple-mix and mulch, as you know. He's also pulled his car around to the bulk landscaping materials area to have purchased bags of manure and loam put into his trunk when he's only needed a couple of bags." He scanned his memory. "We also delivered and planted a number of mature oak and hemlock trees a few years back." It was evident that he had run the gamut of everything he knew about Platson.

"That's true," intoned Jane. "And I've helped him with his selection of perennials and shrubs, on occasion. Working with him can be a bit time-consuming because he's so meticulous about picking the right cultivar, but it helps that we have our perennials organized by their Latin names. We can usually find the one he's looking for." She paused and considered. "I think he does a lot of research on the Internet to find the perfect plant for his garden. It's an unusual approach. He often comes with list in hand. I guess it's better than searching up and down the aisles trying to figure out plant selections on the spot, especially if you're very picky. Most of our shoppers just want some color and easily decide right then and there. Stanford's never been like that. He's very precise."

Marilee mulled these comments over and stored them for later review. She thanked them both for their insights and they returned to the business of the day.

"Jane, when Jaz arrives, please check that she's okay. Finding a dead body has got to be one of the most unpleasant surprises a person could ever experience. If she needs a few days off, that's okay. I prefer that she come back to work when she's ready." Marilee said, a look of concern on her face.

"Yes, I was concerned, too. I drove her home myself on Monday, and checked in with her yesterday. She was still shaken, but she's coping well. I think she'll be all right. When I called her yesterday to let her know we'd be reopening today, she said she would be fine to come back to work. She said she would rather continue with her regular routine than sit at home with nothing to think about than Stanford Platson's lifeless eyes staring at her from his expressionless face."

That makes sense, Marilee thought. *I would be the same. Who wants to sit at home looking at the four walls with nothing to think about but a murder you just witnessed?* It was a somewhat simplistic view, she knew, as people did not actually sit around, but rather took the opportunity to complete chores, laundry, dishes and such, but still the mind recognized that you weren't carrying out your normal routine and continued to revisit the reason for the change. It was an odd habit the mind had, but unfortunately (or fortunately?) it was true. She nodded, acknowledging Jane's update about Jaz's wishes, and was pleased that Jaz would be at work later in the morning. She looked forward to seeing her.

"I'm glad I wasn't the one who found him. That would have been a fright, not that I'm glad that Jaz found him, either. I'm just relieved Jaz is okay," said Pete. Marilee echoed the feeling. *Thank goodness,* thought Marilee, *everything is back to normal.*

~

In the afternoon, Marilee decided it was time to pay her respects to Mrs. Platson. If she was being truthful with herself, Marilee was curious about this woman she'd rarely seen, certainly not in recent years, and the visit was more about fulfilling her curiosity than it was about offering her condolences. She realized that wasn't very charitable of her, and hoped her curiosity wouldn't be too evident.

She grabbed her car keys and headed out of her office. Passing through the shelves of ceramics and creative garden art, Marilee thought it would be nice to arrive at Mrs. Platson's house bringing something cheery to brighten her day. And conveniently, Marilee had access to a broad selection of such things! She picked a beautiful basket of bright yellow daffodils and two-toned peach and white narcissus from a bench near the cash register.

Perfect! Marilee thought. *This is sure to lift Mrs. Platson's spirits.* She headed briskly towards the exit.

"Justin," she called out. Justin was once again staffing the cash register. He looked up from punching in a purchase. "If anybody's looking for me, I'll be reachable on my cell phone," she explained. "I'll be back soon." And with that she headed towards her car.

~

Stanford and Glenda Platson's home proved to be more difficult to find than Marilee had expected. After a number of false turns, Marilee rolled into a quiet cul-de-sac on the other side of town. The houses were predominantly Tudor style two-story homes, about twenty years old, on large, well-established properties. You could tell that the neighborhood residents were fastidious about keeping their gardens and yards well appointed. *Stanford certainly lived in the right neighborhood,* thought Marilee. *His neighbors seem to be cut from the same cloth.* She giggled to herself. *Without knowing it, they're probably egging each other to greater and greater heights,* she mused. *Must make for interesting garden parties. On the plus side,* she observed appreciatively, *I've never seen* such a wonderful sight. It must be the most beautifully landscaped area in town.

She pulled her car to the curb and stopped in front of the Platson house, surveying it from the road. From what she could see, all of the curtains were drawn tight and no sign of human movement was evident from the street. *I wonder if she's home,* Marilee considered. *I should have called ahead; otherwise this may well end up being a wasted trip* .She sighed. *There's no point sitting here guessing. The only way to find out is by ringing the doorbell.*

Marilee stepped out of her car and headed up the driveway. It had been professionally done in an exquisite antique paving stone, in a mottled gray pattern that gave the impression that the stones had been placed decades before. Many homeowners that could afford such a lavish investment chose this type of driveway finish. It was expensive, but created a wonderful feeling of a well-established, old homestead that gave the property an immediate feeling of coziness and comfort.

As she approached the front stoop, she noticed a slight movement, as a curtain swayed and fell back into place in what Marilee took to be the front sitting room. *I should have brought someone with me,* she though nervously. *Nonsense, don't be such a chicken,* she told herself. She rang the doorbell.

A moment's silence followed, then sounds of movement from inside the house. A moment later, Mrs. Platson opened the door. "Yes?" she asked. Looking at the flower basket she nodded her head in the direction of a red brick house on the other side of the street. "If you're the neighborhood welcoming committee, you're looking for the Fletchers. They just moved in last week. They're at number 17 on the other side of the street." She moved to close the door without waiting for confirmation that her assumption was correct.

"Actually, I came to see you, Mrs. Platson. I was hoping you'd recognize me. I'm Marilee Bright, from Green Horizons Garden Center. You used to shop there with your husband, Stanford. I wanted to drop by and let you know how sorry we all are about his unfortunate and untimely passing." Marilee looked sympathetically at Mrs. Platson and glanced down at the basket. "I brought you this in hopes of brightening your day. You can put them on your deck or patio. They're hardy enough to be outside." Marilee added, smiling broadly.

"You might as well come in," Mrs. Platson replied amenably, recovering quickly from her error. "And, please, call me Glenda."

Marilee respectfully slipped out of her shoes and padded after Glenda into the kitchen. It was immediately apparent that the west-facing kitchen gave onto the back yard, and light angled in through the large picture window.

Mrs. Platson was a thin, pale woman with a mass of wiry dark hair held tightly by a flat silver barrette at the nape of her neck. She wore a black pair of slacks that were slightly loose in the rear, showing signs that she had likely lost some weight since having purchased them. A long sleeved faint red blouse rounded out the outfit, the faded color of which indicated that she had worn and washed it many times.

"I'm sorry for being rude. I didn't realize you were looking for me." Glenda said, peering at Marilee over the top of her out-dated, gold-rimmed glasses. "Thank you very much for the gift basket and your kind words. It's nice to have someone drop by. The house seems so empty now that Stanford is gone." She glanced wistfully around her. Her gaze moved to the window and a blank expression crossed her face. She gave the impression that before Marilee arrived, she had been sitting in that very chair, looking vacantly into the yard for hours.

If she's not a grieving widow, she sure puts on a good act, Marilee thought.

"You have a wonderful view," said Marilee. Suddenly, she realized that she had no idea what she was going to say. *You should have thought of that before,* she chided herself. *Now you're in it.* Quickly she returned to the one thing that she knew they had in common.

"I'm sorry about Stanford," she said, for a second time. "He was a frequent visitor to Green Horizons, as you know. He was well liked by the whole staff," she added, somewhat stretching the truth. "His interest in gardening was extensive."

"Yes," muttered Mrs. Platson. "I used to be interested, too, but you know, sometimes you can have enough of a good thing," she explained. "I lost interest a few years ago. People change." she said apologetically. She paused. "Were you the person who found him?" she asked, clearly pained.

"No. Actually, one of my staff did. Jaz is her name."

"It must have been quite a fright for her," she continued. She paused again. "You know, Stanford and I were married for thirty-two years. In some ways it seems like forever, and in some ways it seems like such a short time." She sighed.

"Are you planning to stay in this house?" asked Marilee inquisitively, hoping that Glenda wouldn't notice the abrupt change in topic. "It seems very large for just one person."

"Yes, you're right. I'm thinking of selling and moving to something more manageable. Stanford used to do all of the yard work, and now that I'm alone, I won't be able to manage it. I could hire a yard maintenance company, but, frankly, it's not worth it, and I don't want to spend the rest of my life surrounded by memories of my life with Stanford. Not because I didn't love him," she added quickly, "because I did. Very much so. But the memories in this house are too much for me now. I'll be moving as soon as I've decided where I plan to live and have sold the house. I may move away from this area," Glenda explained. "Maybe to Florida, or Georgia. Did you know my son, Robert, lives in Florida with his wife and three kids?" Glenda's voice took on a more animated tone. "He's a bank manager. Takes after his father that way. Always had a good head for numbers. And my daughter, Evelyn, lives in Georgia. She's a fashion magazine editor, and just got engaged to an architect. Sorry, I'm blathering." She paused, embarrassed.

Picking up on the stream of information flowing from Glenda, Marilee said, "It must have been a great shock to you when you were informed of Stanford's death."

Glenda cast her eyes downward, either in a move to appear sorrowful, or to hide another, more sinister, emotion. "Yes, of course, how could I not be? He was a good husband, despite our recent differences."

The statement begged for clarification. "What differences?" Marilee asked innocently. *Let's see what she says to that one.*

"Like I said, we used to have similar interests, you know, and spend time together. Recently, we had developed different interests. I was more interested in spending time with my friends. Stan has never tired of his interest in gardening, and wanted to spend every waking moment either on his garden or on his garden pictures. When he wasn't at work, of course." She smiled thinly. "My friends and I play bridge on Tuesdays, and I've made a habit of Saturday bingo and occasional bowling. I've just joined a league," she explained.

"Getting together with your friends should help break the tedium of being alone in this big house." Marilee said brightly. "Do you do any work outside the home?"

"Yes, that's been a great release, as well," acknowledged Glenda. "I work part-time at the Teasdale library branch on Fisher Street."

Marilee had a sudden thought. How was Glenda going to get along financially now that Stanford was gone? Tactfully she said, "That sounds like a great place to work. I've been there. Will you be able to continue the same hours?" She hoped it was a tactful way of asking whether Glenda would be forced to work full-time to support herself, or whether a large insurance payment was in the offing.

Glenda did not look at her directly. "If I move out of town, I'll have to give that up now, won't I?"

~

After Marilee had said her good byes and wished Glenda well, she returned to the store.

Pete and Jane were thankful of her return and accosted her as soon as she set foot inside the entranceway.

Jane was the first to speak. "I'm sorry Marilee, but we could sure use a hand with the receiving. The shipments that weren't delivered yesterday arrived this afternoon along with today's scheduled deliveries and we're having a challenge keeping up. Will you have some time to help us bring out and organize the perennial flats?" she asked hopefully. She looked frazzled. Wisps of hair were plastered to her face and smudges of dirt lined her forehead.

"Before you get to that," Pete asked hopefully, "a shipment of five dozen columnar cedars arrived this afternoon. I don't have any paperwork on this shipment. Do you have anything? I hope you do, because there wasn't much I could do except sign for the delivery. The shipper wasn't willing to leave without having delivered it. I hope it's not a problem, Marilee." Pete was exasperated with the situation, Marilee could tell. He was easily agitated by unexpected events, and didn't like confusion. He liked everything to go as planned.

"No problem, to both of your questions," responded Marilee. "First, Pete, I'll stop by the office and take a look for that purchase order. Then, Jane, I'll head right out to help you and Jaz with the perennials. Is everyone okay with that?" Both Pete and Jane nodded, looking relieved. *That's what I'm here for,* thought Marilee, pleased to have been able to help sort things.

Marilee headed back to her office, but many thoughts were competing in her mind. Her visit with Glenda Platson had been mysterious and somewhat enlightening, although she had not received any insight into the question of a life insurance settlement. But it made her think that Glenda had more than one reason to rid herself of Stanford. Marilee decided that she would give more thought to that later, once the shipments had been straightened out and the perennials had been received and sorted for sale.

The rest of the afternoon passed productively, with everyone back on track with receiving, pricing, sorting and setting out of various incoming shipments.

Justin was busy ringing in customer purchases and barely had a moment to lend a hand. As one of the regular staff, Justin had worked at the garden center every year for the past three years from the day his university exams ended in early April to his return to school in September. He was a great help and Marilee trusted him to run the cash with a minimum of supervision. These days, most people paid with credit or debit cards, and Justin was skilled and knowledgeable about the correct charging procedures. In fact, very few people paid by cash anymore. The cost of garden center purchases had risen like anything else, and very few people left having spent only ten or twenty dollars for their purchases.

Jane, Marilee, Jaz and Tracey worked on retrieving the perennials from one of the greenhouses where they were kept until prepared for sale and space became available on the racks.

They worked quickly, side by side, first retrieving trays of fragrant Sweet William, perennial flax, Johnson's Blue Cranesbill, sturdy pink bergenia and turtlehead to the display shelves. They ensured each pot contained a live plant, removing dead leaves and spent blooms as they went. They also checked that each container was equipped with a descriptive plant tag.

Plant tags were provided by the supplier and served several purposes. First, they provided a picture of the mature plant, including blooms, if important. Second, they detailed what height and width the plant would eventually occupy in the garden. Third, they provided details about the plant's environment preferences, such as sun and shade tolerance, type of soil and water requirements. Lastly, the nursery's name was identified as the grower. That was a lot of information for such a small tag, and the size of the tags had grown in recent years to accommodate all of the information that a gardener would want to know before selecting a perennial for their garden flowerbeds.

Often these tags were simple narrow, tapered plastic tags that were stabbed into the soil. As these tags were prone to falling out or being removed by customers, some growers had adopted plant tags with upwards facing hooks that were slipped into slots on the outsides of containers, making them difficult to remove, both inadvertently or intentionally.

The new design had become a major time-saver and also prevented the garden center from having to hold "surprise" discount sales in which a number of unlabelled plants were offered at hugely discounted prices. The surprise was that you only learned what the plant was if you could identify it, or once it had matured in your garden. Not many gardeners were that adventurous, and it did the garden center's finances no good to have to mark down perfectly good plants just because the identification tag was missing.

After checking the tags, the team ensured that like plants were placed together with like plants on the trays, checked the pot color (pot color and size dictated the price that was charged at the check-out) and placed the perennials in alphabetical order on the shelves for customers to peruse and select.

It was a busy yet fun time, and the four women shared a few laughs and tales of their lives.

"So what did everyone do this winter?" asked Jane.

"I went to visit my family in England," said Jaz. "As you know, my parents live in Birmingham, and they look forward to my visits. But I don't stay long, as my husband can't get away from his work at that time, and the kids are in school."

"So same as usual," chided Jane. "I think you've done the same thing for the past ten years!" she exclaimed.

"Yes," said Jaz holding up a periwinkle bursting with strands of mauve flower buds, "but it's great to see them, especially since my husband is not keen on them. This way, he has the perfect excuse not to come along. Also, I like to get provisions that are uniquely English that I can't find here."

"Don't your kids miss you?" asked Tracey. "My kids would be frantic. They'd be afraid I wasn't coming back."

Jaz laughed. "My kids are old enough now to understand. Don't forget, Marie is 13 and Robert is 15. They know how to take care of themselves." She checked the tags on a number of Black-eyed Susan plants. Black-eyed Susans, a popular member of the daisy flower and a relative of purple coneflower (latin name, Echinacea), from which the popular health remedy was derived, came in a variety of sizes and colors, although predominantly in the golden tones. "My, these are going to be beautiful," she said showing them the plant. "I bought some of these last year, and they were just lovely. I think I'll have to put aside a couple of these for my garden. And, do you know what? I noticed last year that the finches eat the seeds in the winter, and a couple more plants would help feed them," She said, pleased that her purchases would not only brighten her garden, but also feed the wild bird life over the long winter months.

"Of course," replied Marilee. "Just put them aside and Justin can ring them through for you later. Don't forget to use your employee discount card." It was one of the innovations Marilee had instituted when she had bought the business. It just made sense to her that her employees should be able to create gardens that reflected their work. It would be a sorry sight if garden center employees had guests at their homes and they had no garden to speak of! Everyone had enthusiastically endorsed the move and many had thanked her for thinking of them. It was the most popular employee benefit the garden center offered.

"My husband and I took the kids to Epcot Center over Christmas," said Jane. "It was great. The kids had a great time, and my husband and

I enjoyed the trip too. After we got back, I spent a couple of weeks with my brother in Sedona, Arizona. He's a golf instructor," she explained.

"That sounds great," said Tracey. "I didn't do much, but it was great to be able to spend more time with my kids and husband. You know, the kids grow up so fast, and these winter breaks let me devote more time to them. For the rest of the year, they head over to their grandmother's after school until either Doug or I get home." She chuckled. "I know she'd never say so, but I bet she appreciates getting a break from the kids, too. I'm sure they never give her a moment's rest from the minute they arrive to the minute Doug or I pick them up."

They all laughed. It was great to be able to talk and get caught up with each other's lives while they worked.

~

That evening Marilee enjoyed a glass of wine at home, her feet resting on an overstuffed ottoman.

She lived in a small red brick bungalow on an irregular shaped lot, not far from Green Horizons, situated on a quiet suburban street populated by a variety of families. The south-facing house was simply laid out: to the west of a broad central oak-floored hallway lay a west-facing kitchen (with eat-in breakfast nook) and living room. To the east lay two rectangular bedrooms bracketing a small main bath. When she had originally acquired the garden center she had commuted from her existing home in the suburbs for the first couple of years. After contacting local real estate agents to find a small-sized home in or near Sandalwood, she had hit pay dirt. For her, the house and layout were perfect and the ideal size for her and her cat, Cinder. Marilee loved the afternoon light in the kitchen. It made everything so cozy; the feel of the warmed ceramic tiles underfoot and the gold sunrays streaming into the room were delightful. The home was tastefully painted with earth-tone shades that included pale yellow, moss green, pumpkin, terra cotta and mocha colors. They added a relaxing feel to the place, making it a peaceful retreat from the world.

In the mornings, the early glow of the sun through her translucent window shades helped get Marilee started on her day. Winter times were tougher, but it helped that Marilee spent a majority of that time in the southern US. Here, cool nighttime temperatures made one want to snuggle deeper into one's comforter rather than venture a tentative toe out into the frigid air.

Cinder was a beautiful British Blue with gray-green eyes. He was also Marilee's constant companion, and followed her with interest from room to room. Seemingly, he never failed to be entertained, even when alone during the day, for Marilee had never seen him express the slightest interest in the outside world. He was perfectly happy to watch the birds from an indoor window perch, which was fine with Marilee. She preferred knowing where he was at all times, and would have been worried sick if he had ever ventured outside. Thankfully, he wasn't the type to loiter around doors in the hopes that someone carelessly opened one so he could slip out unnoticed.

At the moment, Marilee was installed in her cozy living room, relaxing on the matching overstuffed sofa, in front of the unlit stone fireplace. The sun had already set, and a chill had set in. She was cuddled up with a soft fleece burgundy throw across her legs and Cinder installed comfortably on her lap. Daytime temperatures had warmed up significantly from a month ago, but evenings were still nippy. Marilee was loath to light the fireplace, however. It seemed silly that the first time she'd start it up this year would be April. That didn't sit right with her. So, instead, she had retrieved the blanket from her small hall closet where she stored tablecloths, extra towels and, of course, blankets.

She pulled up her knees to form an inverted "V" with her legs, jostling Cinder slightly (who didn't seem to mind), and grabbed a paper and pen from a nearby occasional table. She reached across to adjust the table lamp to a higher setting. Again she was thinking about Stanford Platson's murder. It was occupying a great deal of her mind and it bothered her that she still didn't know much more than she had at the beginning. Her meeting with Glenda had raised more questions than answers. In some ways, Glenda appeared truly stricken by her husband's death. On the other hand, she seemed to have a well-established independent life, and it appeared that she would be able to exist comfortably without him. In addition, there was a strange dichotomy between Glenda's circle of friends and her statement that she might move to Florida or Georgia. If she had such a close network of friends, why was she willing to start fresh somewhere new?

Marilee paused. *Was it possible that Glenda had met someone through her bridge or bowling club and the two of them were planning to get married, or at least move in together, and live in another state?* Now that was an interesting thought. That would fit, thought Marilee. She reassessed Glenda Platson. How old was she? Maybe in her early or mid fifties? Her gaunt, pale face and severe hair style did not make her appear all that attractive, but there's no accounting for taste, she reminded herself. Maybe when she gets all done up she looks all right. She almost slapped herself. Here I go, perpetuating the view that a woman's value to a man was all about her looks. Not every relationship is about looks, she reminded herself sternly. Compatibility between individuals is what counts. Things like shared interests and compatible personalities, for example. She paused. Okay, looks help too, she admitted grudgingly.

Marilee drummed her pen on her knee and took another sip of wine. Mmm, Chardonnay, one of her favorites. She gazed at the wine in her glass. It had a rich gold tone. The light from her reading lamp sparkled on the wine's smooth surface.

She mulled over the facts she had learned since she had started her unofficial investigation into Platson's death, while she petted Cinder affectionately. She, Marilee, knew now that he was a financial controller at a local roofing company. Maybe he had found some accounting irregularities in the books? Was the head honcho cooking the books, and Platson had become aware of it after being promoted to controller? Was it something as simple as that? It wouldn't be the first time something like that had happened.

She closed her eyes as Cinder purred contentedly on her lap, and gradually drifted off to sleep. The last thought that crossed her mind was that it was probably not the best plan to drink alcohol while racking your brain to solve a mystery.

Chapter 6

▼

The following morning brought a visit from George, and Jim, who had also attended the crime scene on Monday.

"Hi again," said Marilee to the two police officers.

"Hi there, Marilee," said George. Jim nodded in acknowledgment of the greeting but kept silent.

"By the way, George, when are you and your wife, Vivian, going to come by to check out this year's new plants?" teased Marilee. "It's a bit early for annuals, but I hear that a new cascading petunia is being introduced this year. It is said to flower all summer with huge, pink, purple or white-striped purple double blooms.

Also, this year's 'Perennial of the Year' has been announced, and I'm happy to say we'll be stocking up on it to ensure that everyone has a chance to buy one. It's called Rozanne Cranesbill Geranium, and it's perfect for containers, window boxes and raised planters. The flowers are large violet-blue with purple-violet veins. I hear it has one of the longest flowering periods, and will not need to be pruned or deadheaded. Sounds wonderful, doesn't it? I'm planning to buy a few myself. The first shipment will arrive on Monday, if Vivian's interested.

Will you let her know?" Marilee looked expectantly at George. "You won't forget, will you? I know she'll be interested."

George sighed, not as excited by the new plant introduction as Marilee clearly was. "I guess you'll give me a hard time if I forget, and you'll rub it in the next time I come by," he said jovially. "I'll make a note." And he dutifully took out his police notepad and made a note to tell Vivian to give Marilee a call about this year's new plant offerings. His note was succinct. It was impossible for him to write down everything that Marilee had just said. Anyway, this gave Vivian a good excuse to call Marilee and get caught up on recent events in their lives. "Got it," he said, putting away his pad.

"But that's not why I came," he said, recalling the reason for his visit. "I came to let you know that we've finished the forensic search of Stanford's car, and retrieved all of the possessions he had with him at the time of his death. We were looking for any sign that he had made arrangements to meet someone at Green Horizons, some note, some scrap of paper, or a business card, showing a name. Or a phone number, date and time. Something like that." He looked tired. "I don't mind telling you that we found nothing, but please don't go discussing the details of what has and has not been found, with your staff." Marilee nodded in acceptance of his terms.

He continued. "The interesting thing is what we did not find. We learned from Mrs. Platson that her husband was in the habit of carrying a small digital camera with him wherever he went. When we searched his pockets, we found a camera. Mrs. Platson has identified the camera as his. That's not surprising. What is surprising is that the memory card is missing from the camera." He looked at Marilee quizzically. "Did you happen to remove it when you went to check the body after Jaz found him?" Jim carefully watched Marilee's reaction. He was suspicious of everyone.

"My goodness, no, I did not. I didn't touch a thing." Marilee responded, shocked. "I just checked whether he had a pulse, and if there was anything we could do for the poor man, like administer First Aid," she explained. "I hope you don't take me for an idiot," she said. "I know how important it is not to mess with the scene of a crime!" Once she had considered his question a moment more, Marilee became indignant at the accusation, although she knew they were just doing their duty.

"Yes, I thought as much. Sorry, Marilee, I didn't mean to offend you. You know how it is. I have to ask," he said apologetically. *Damn, it's awkward investigating a murder when it happens in your own backyard. It's difficult not to damage your relationships with your friends and acquaintances,* he thought to himself. He sighed. Well, at least his skills at tactful questioning of witnesses were improving. He glanced sideways at Jim, thinking he could benefit from improved tact as well.

"Jim and I will need to speak with Jaz again," he said. "Is she around? I hope you don't mind us occupying your break room again. We won't be long."

Marilee headed out to find Jaz. Was Jaz a suspect?? Marilee hadn't even thought of it! She doubted it. Jaz had no reason to murder Stanford or to take a memory card from his camera. She doubted she even had the strength to drive a cultivator into Stanford's chest. But, at the same time, she acknowledged that their work was very physical, and each of them had well developed upper body strength from lifting and moving plants and shrubs all day. And, of course, she was the person who found Platson's body. Could it be that she actually encountered him *alive,* but left him behind, dead? But, no, Jaz wouldn't hurt a fly.

It was with these thoughts floating around in her mind that she found Jaz pricing white cedars in the evergreen lot. She briefly explained that George and Jim were back to question her. To minimize nervousness on Jaz's part, Marilee made light of the situation, and they talked about the quality of this year's magnolia tree crop as they made their way back to the office and into the lunchroom, where the two detectives greeted Jaz. Marilee closed the door discretely and returned, worried, to her office.

~

Things were becoming intense! She retrieved the note pad from her desk that she had made a few notes on before.

The first thing she did was to change the heading. She struck out "Motives" and replaced it with "Suspects".

Under "Suspects" she wrote "Glenda Platson". By now, Marilee had a number of reasons to suspect the widow Platson. Marilee added details under her name. Life insurance was still her favorite motive, and now she added others: a possible lover, a desire to move out of state, and a desire to cash in the house to finance these lifestyle changes. She could see now that divorce would not have been as lucrative; she would have had to split the value of the house and other assets with Stanford. Stanford's death meant a bigger bank account with which Glenda could pursue any number of new lifestyles.

Marilee sighed. *How sad that anyone would come to the conclusion that one's spouse, while alive, was hampering one's pocketbook,* she thought.

If the killer was Glenda Platson, why had she chosen such a violent, public way to kill her husband? There must be any number of ways she could have killed him without doing it in such a brutal and public manner! As his wife, she would have had ample opportunity to kill him at home. She could have poisoned his soup, for example, or pushed him down the stairs.

She moved on to other possible suspects. Much as she didn't want to, she added Jaz's name to the list. To Marilee, Jaz was not a likely suspect but she had to admit that Jaz had the opportunity; she was in the same spot as the living Stanford had been standing moments before. Who's to say she didn't wield the weapon that killed him? Marilee thought not, but with a heavy heart she acknowledged that Jaz's name would have to stay on the list for now, not that she had the faintest idea what a possible motive could be.

What about the missing camera memory card? How did that fit into the picture? What could have possibly been on the card? From what she had heard, Platson took pictures of flowers. Flowers? What was so sinister about flowers?? She chuckled. That was it; it was a big sinister flower plot! Case solved. She sighed. Okay, that wasn't the solution. Think, think, she told herself.

On the pad, she wrote 'Co-worker/boss'. The killer could also be a business acquaintance. Marilee added this to the list as well. *This is not good,* she mumbled to herself. *Now I have a growing list of possible suspects, but no real supporting evidence.* She resolved to look further into possible business reasons for Platson's death.

She headed over to the landscaping office to check in with Trent, Stella and Gene. On the way, she surveyed the displays. Today, Karen was stocking the indoor potting soil shelves with vermiculite and specialty soils for cacti, African violets and tropical plants. Thankfully, the soil bags were small; otherwise they would have been quite heavy. Marilee stopped to chat with her, which was her way of providing a small break to her staff. Karen seemed relieved at the interruption.

"How is it going?" asked Marilee. "I see you've got the indoor soil shelves well stocked. Do you find that people are buying the specialty soil as much as the all-purpose indoor soil?"

Karen considered for a moment. "Yes, actually, I think all of the indoor soils are selling well, based on my restocking activities. People seem to appreciate that we stock the specialty soils, and seem to know that, for example, African violet soil is the best type of soil for African violets. I think they've learned over the years that all-purpose soil doesn't produce as healthy a plant and as many flowers." She pointed at the neighboring fertilizers. "These seem to be very popular too. We don't seem to be able to keep them on the shelf!" She brushed the back of her hand across her forehead.

Marilee was pleased with the update. Of course, she knew full well which of her products sold and which ones did not, as she did the purchasing, but she enjoyed consulting with her staff. It also gave her some insight into who paid attention to the business, and who did not. Clearly Karen was an astute observer of the buying habits of their clientele and Marilee made a mental note of this capability for future reference. You never knew when you would need to rely on someone's expertise.

She continued over the tiled floor past the shelves of mirrored gazing balls, colorful glazed vases, whimsical wind chimes, gardening gloves and solar-powered garden lights to the landscaping office. The woodpaneled area was basically a large open room that was accessed from the indoor display area. Within the landscaping office, three nooks were separated from each other by half-walls, and each contained a desk where the designers provided consulting services to clients.

Behind each desk stood a well-used chair, and in front were two fabric guest chairs. The entire color scheme was one of earth tones, reflecting the office's use: warm terra cotta colored seating was accompanied by the muted tawny of the desks and walls. Deep green metal credenzas lined the walls behind each desk chair. The half-walls were a soft taupe. In contrast to the natural colors of the room, a silver-colored computer with a black flat panel screen containing landscape design software occupied a corner of each desk.

Covering much of the wall space in each nook were landscape drawings representing each designer's current and favorite design projects, and brochures and sample landscaping materials, interlocking pavers and such, covered every available surface. As she finished surveying the room, her eyes rested on a small cabinet near the door where half full coffee carafe stood in a drip-style coffee maker. Marilee eyeballed the carafe and wondered how old the coffee was. She decided to pass. Anyway, she had her own coffee maker in her office, and she knew her coffee was fresh, as she had made it a few minutes ago.

Stella was deep in discussions with some customers. Marilee recognized them. It was Mr. and Mrs. Whitson. The two parties, Green Horizons and the Whitsons, had been discussing the Whitsons' front landscape design on and off for the last two years. It was always a challenge to transform a piece of land from its current status to something new. It was not the loss of the current condition that eluded clients, for that part of the change was desirable, but rather designing something new to the exclusion of all other possibilities, that was always the challenge.

Gene was nowhere to be seen. Presumably he was on-site consulting with a client. It was a frequent occurrence that one or all of the designers were off visiting their clients to observe the orientation of the lot to the sun, and grading and drainage issues that were not easily identified without a site visit. Clients were notorious for failing to recognize these potential problem areas. For these reason, it was always a good idea to visit the grounds before committing any design ideas to paper.

Trent was wrapping up. Marilee decided to wait until he became available. To occupy her time, she picked up a brochure from a stone supplier and leafed through the handful of colorful pages showing potential stone uses.

It wasn't long before Trent and his visitor said their good-byes. "I'll give you a call next week when I have some suggestions for the materials we can use for your new retaining wall," she could hear him say as he handed him a business card with his contact information. As the client left, he gave Marilee a quick nod before stepping out of the landscaping office.

Trent glanced at Marilee as he gathered his notes together. Marilee went over and sat in one of the guest chairs.

"Everything going okay?" she asked.

"Yeah, no problem. Jack Shilling wants to build a retaining wall in his yard, to avoid soil erosion around his roses. It may be a costly venture, but I think it's the right answer for his problem. I promised to give him a call next week with some suggestions." He looked at Marilee inquisitively. "What's eating you?"

"I keep thinking about the murder of Stanford Platson. Somehow, because it happened at Green Horizons, I feel responsible for what happened. And I can't believe there's someone in our community who would do such a thing. To think that we have a murderer running around. How do we know the killer won't do it again?" She threw a concerned look his way, lowering her voice low so that the Whitsons could not hear. "I mean, we're assuming the killer targeted Stanford specifically, but what if we're wrong?"

"You're scaring me," responded Trent. "Although what you say is possible. But what are we supposed to do, stay at home with the doors locked until the perpetrator is behind bars? That's not a very practical solution."

They both considered the implications of Marilee's comment for a moment.

"Are you planning to warn everyone of this possibility, Marilee?" asked Trent in a concerned tone. "Somehow I think that will do more harm than good. All you'll succeed in doing is scaring the bejeezers out of everyone, and we'll be no further ahead."

Marilee chewed the inside of her cheek as she thought about Trent's insights. "Hmmm," she said.

"Wouldn't it be great if we knew something about the killer and could lure him into a trap?" she asked, a note of excitement creeping into her voice.

Trent shook his head vigorously. "Yikes, Marilee! That sounds dangerous to me. Anyway, what do you know about the killer that you could use to lure him? And, might I remind you that this is what we pay our local police officers for. They're the ones who are supposed to be carrying out the dangerous killer-catching work!"

Marilee could see the logic in the arguments that Trent had raised. She eyeballed him playfully. "Gees, you're taking all my fun away. Don't you know I'm a closet detective?" She winked at him. "I guess you're not in support of that idea," she capitulated belatedly. "As it is, I don't have any clue who the killer is, so I guess he's safe from me for now."

Chapter 7

▼

The following weekend was the regional home show. Green Horizons had been planning for the event since the previous fall, contemplating booth display designs and looking through catalogues of potential promotional items. The three-day event started on Friday morning. Trent, Jaz and Marilee had arranged to meet in the Green Horizons parking lot. Marilee could see Trent and Jaz standing by the garden center entrance, waiting for her, as she pulled into the driveway. They left the rest of the team to run the store while they headed to the nearby arena where the event would take place. Pete was point person for any issues, and she told him to call her if they needed to reach any one of them.

They piled into her three year old Toyota FJ Cruiser. When she had bought it used, the dealership had described the color as 'Burnt Sunset'. Whatever they called it, Marilee loved it. It was a metallic, rusty-orange color and was unique enough to be a little off the beaten track, which she thought was perfect, as she considered herself a little off the beaten track as well. The vehicle ran well and was surprisingly fuel-efficient.

As they belted themselves in, each checked that they had all of the necessary supplies with them: business cards, garden center brochures, pens and note pads and promotional items to hand out to attendees and potential clients. This year, they would hand out wild-flower seed packets as well as magnetic calendars showing a snapshot of the garden center and listing its phone number and location. They had purchased a thousand of each, hoping that that would last them for the length of the show. Trent also checked that he had all of the paperwork documenting the arrangements he had made so that if anything were awry when they got to their booth, they would hopefully be able to straighten it out on the spot with the show's organizers.

As they arrived at the arena parking lot, the place was already filling with other exhibitors ready to start their day. Many had arrived in the early hours to assemble their displays. They had been unable to access the building yesterday to set up; at other times the arena was booked with roller-blade hockey and lacrosse games, as well as with other events. Marilee was impressed: some exhibitors had elaborate display booths. The objective was to draw the greatest crowds and hopefully make lasting impressions on the throngs of potential customers, and installers had just one more hour to get everything in place.

The Green Horizons staff quickly jumped out of the SUV and headed inside to find their booth. The arena was a perfect venue for the regional home show. The huge space and high ceiling allowed for a large number of exhibitors and easily accommodated their elaborate displays. Thankfully, in foresight, the organizers had spaced the aisles widely, permitting the fluid movement of interested attendees past the series of vendor booths without causing problematic bottlenecks.

They found their booth without any problems. Trent was right; it was in a perfect spot. It was near the only concession stand and located at the end of an aisle near the entrance, making it pretty hard to miss.

"Good job," said Marilee. Trent was delighted. He thought so, too. They moved quickly to complete any last minute preparations, which included a number of steps, including checking that the display they had hired installers to assemble that morning had been correctly put together. No one wanted the display to fall on him or her in the middle of the show! Or God forbid, have it crumble on top of the attending public, which would cause a real nightmare. They laid out business cards and promotional materials on a tall, narrow rectangular table in preparation for the onslaught of expected visitors.

Excitement ran through their veins. Marilee felt the adrenaline rush as she waited for the doors to open to the public. It was always an exciting event, and this year's would undoubtedly prove to be just as interesting.

She glanced around her. Since she had learned of Platson's occupation and employer the previous week, she hoped that Sturdy Roofing Installations would have a booth at this year's show, as they had in previous years. If they did, she was going to make a point of dropping by to meet the people staffing the Sturdy booth. Of course, her ulterior motive was to find out more about Stanford and Sturdy's financial situation. However, it was highly unlikely that finances would be discussed at the show. It was an absolute no-no, which made it all the more of a challenge to Marilee's investigative skills. She hoped she could identify which of the Sturdy people would be the easiest to pump for information without them getting the slightest inkling what she was up to. She felt like a clandestine operative.

Unfortunately, from her current vantage point, Marilee could not see the Sturdy booth, if it even existed. She had hoped that she could monitor it while staffing her own booth. It turned out to be wishful thinking. She resolved to tour the show at her first opportunity.

It wasn't long before customers and clients started milling throughout the show. Immediately their booth became a beehive of activity. People loved landscapes and they were eager to find out more about the garden center: What did they sell? Where was it located? Did they also install the landscapes they designed? Did they carry hybrid tea/climbing/floribunda/miniature roses? The barrage of questions continued unabated until shortly before 10 o'clock when Marilee noticed that she and Jaz had a brief respite from the crowd. Trent was deep in discussions with a potential customer, and was sketching some quick ideas that would hopefully motivate the customer to engage Green Horizons' designers. She whispered to Jaz, "I'm going for a quick bathroom break. I'll be right back." Jaz nodded as she slumped, exhausted, into the only available chair and took a sip of bottled water.

Marilee headed through the aisles of show booths, greeting people and vendors as she went. She had to keep focused, however, or she would get mired in the usual meet-and-greet and would fail to achieve her real objective. She hurried along. She would be surprised if Sturdy had opted out of attending this year, but she had yet to see their booth. *That's odd,* she thought. It cost only a few hundred dollars to attend, and the exposure to new business was definitely worth it. That stream of thought ended, however, when she spied the shingled Sturdy Roofing Installations sign over the throng of attendees.

As she approached the booth, she checked to see whether she recognized anyone at the booth. Charles Kingly was the company president. She hoped that she would recognize him, as she had researched the company on the Internet and had come across his picture on Sturdy's Web site. Hopefully, she would run into him, although she had not exactly figured out what she would say and how the conversation would go.

Instead, she was instantly greeted by a sales representative (go figure), who identified herself as Holly Traney as she aggressively handed Marilee her business card. Holly was evidently intent on drumming up new business. "We do residential, industrial and commercial roofing," she explained. "Are you currently in the market for a new roof?" Marilee recognized the question for what it was. It meant 'are you going to result in an immediate sale for me or am I wasting my time talking to you'.

Marilee considered whether she should take on the deceitful role of potential customer or to be semi-honest about her purpose in dropping by the booth. She decided to go with the semi-honest approach.

"Hi, Holly," she said, "I'm Marilee Bright from Green Horizons," she paused as the penny dropped.

"Oh my gosh," Holly gasped. "That's where our controller, Stanford Platson, was killed!" she lowered her voice, realizing that she was disturbing nearby customers. "Oh, my goodness. That must have been awful. I mean finding him in your rose bushes." Marilee forgave the erroneousness of Holly's facts. Holly scrunched up her nose. "Eew, did you find him?" she whispered, clearly curious for the gory details and forgetting all about business. Marilee did not answer, other than to clarify that she had, in fact, not been the one to find him. In contrast to Holly, she did not want to revisit the gory details.

"Yes, it was very startling for the staff at Green Horizons to find that someone had been killed at our garden center." Marilee responded. "I wonder what motive anyone would have to kill him." She realized that this conversation would be better held away from the booth, and Holly was clearly interested in gossiping about it, so Marilee suggested that they take a walk. After advising her colleagues, Holly headed down the aisle with Marilee.

Marilee waited for Holly to respond to her comment. Thankfully, Holly was nicely accommodating.

"I've got my theories. Would you like to hear them?" she leaned forward conspiratorially, her eyes wide with excitement.

"Sure."

"Promise you won't tell anyone." Marilee nodded. *What kind of a fool makes a total stranger promise not to divulge their conversation, especially when it involves an open police investigation?* thought Marilee. *Evidently Holly is more interested in gossiping than protecting her company's secrets, whatever they were. So much the better for me.* She felt duplicitous and waited for the feeling to pass. *Hey, you can't make an omelet without breaking a few eggs,* she told herself.

"... and then I found Charles Kingly accusing Stanford of embezzling funds from the company. I couldn't help overhearing them one evening." *Sure you couldn't. You probably had a glass pressed against the wall,* thought Marilee skeptically. "I returned to work after hours to pick up some papers for a meeting the following day with a client, and I saw Charles standing in the doorway to Stanford's office, tearing into him, giving him a piece of his mind. He was so worked up, he had to loosen his tie and undo a button so that the blood wouldn't make his head explode." She giggled. "He should try not to get so worked up. He has high blood pressure, you know."

"How do you know it was Stanford in the office?" asked Marilee. "And why was Stanford still working there at the time of his death if he was embezzling? Surely Charles would have fired him on the spot if it was true."

Evidently Holly had never considered these two points, and took a moment to mull them over. "I'm pretty sure it was Stanford. It was his office after all. But you're right, I didn't see him, and, now that I think about it, I don't think I heard him respond. But I'm pretty sure it was him. The following day when I returned from my client meeting around eleven o'clock, I saw them both in the office, and you could tell they were barely on speaking terms." She explained.

"I see." Marilee took a moment to compose her next question. She wanted to know more about the financial stability of the company, but didn't want to be blunt. If she was too forthright, she ran the risk that Holly would get suspicious and repeat their conversation to Charles Kingly, which would likely get Marilee into hot water and result in an unwanted visit from Detective Blackwell.

"So how long have you worked at Sturdy? Do you like it?" she asked innocently.

"I like it okay. I've been there for almost five years, and was promoted into sales after two years, which was great. I don't think I would have had this opportunity if I'd been working elsewhere. The money I make now as a sales representative sure beats the money I was making on the order desk. I guess Charles saw some potential in me and thought I'd be good at sales. Looks like he was right because I'm making good commissions on roofing sales."

She was having a great time talking about herself. Marilee regretted having to end their informative conversation, but it was time that she returned to her booth. Marilee shook Holly's hand and gave her one of the fridge magnet calendars she'd been carrying.

"It was a pleasure to meet you, Holly. Don't be a stranger. Come by Green Horizons some time. I'm sure we'll be able to find you some plants you'll like."

Holly looked pleased to have been able to share her theories about Stanford Platson with someone, whoever it was. She promised to come by the garden center and chat another time. *She thinks she's made a new friend in me.* Marilee thought, *if she comes by, I'll gladly pick her brain again.* Although Holly may not have had a chance to fully outline her theories, Marilee had learned all she needed to know. There were possibly business related motives linked to Stanford Platson's death, and the business did not seem to be in financial straits, if Holly's comments were anything to go by. And that was all she needed to know for now.

The remainder of the morning and afternoon passed quickly. They barely had time to grab a hotdog at the concession stand for lunch. Then it was back at it.

Some of the people were only interested in receiving a free seed package or calendar, and the supply they had set aside for the day's visitors was gone by mid-afternoon. Others were looking for free advice on plant maintenance. 'Why is my pear tree covered in dark, scaly ulcers?' and 'I can't keep grubs from ruining my grass. What do you recommend?' people asked. Marilee and Jaz did their best to direct them to disease and pest control products offered at Green Horizons.

Many were legitimate potential customers, and Marilee, Jaz and Trent were thrilled that they had enticed some new customers to visit the garden center through the day's efforts.

Later, Trent and Marilee left Jaz in charge of the booth and headed out to see whether any of their competition was attending. Marilee was always surprised to see the diverse businesses that touted their wares at the home show. It was equally astounding how many local businesses even existed in the region. The nation was truly a vast network of small owner-run businesses. It was this fabric that held the economy together, she surmised, not a handful of mass conglomerates.

As they strolled up and down the aisles, Marilee and Trent waved at neighbors and people they knew. There were a number of interior decorators and designers, photographers, sellers of water purification systems, fence and deck installers, financial services firms, people offering their services to perform small handiwork around the house, cabinet and counter makers, as well as doggie training schools and cookware hawkers.

Eventually they happened upon one of their competitors, Grenville Landscaping. Marilee and Grenville's owner, Sandro Valentes, were old acquaintances. It was hard not to know the competition when you often ended up at the same events, such as home and trade shows or conferences. Sandro waved 'hi' as they approached his booth, and asked jokingly whether they were in the market for some landscaping services. "Funny," said Marilee, amused. "How are you keeping, Sandro? I haven't seen you since that trade show back in February. How are your wife and kids?" Sandro had three children, all under the age of twelve.

"Not bad," said Sandro. "Mary has joined the parent-teacher association. She has some great ideas about after school programs and ways to help the students learn to read. The kids are fine, you know, behaving and doing well in school, which is all I can ask. I hear the tough years are ahead of us. I hope we can manage to keep the kids out of trouble, and make sure they get good educations. I'm already saving for the day that my oldest, Ernesto, starts college!" said Sandro with a broad grin. He was definitely a family man.

"Well that's good to hear, Sandro."

"Say, I heard you had some trouble over at your place, a few days ago. Someone was killed?" he didn't bother to lower his voice. What did he care if people no longer wanted to shop at Marilee's garden center? It was potential business for him. He made it sound as if Green Horizons was a dangerous place to work.

"Yes, unfortunately, a long time, loyal customer, Stanford Platson was killed on our premises by an unknown person. I'm sure you read about it in the Sandalwood Chronicle." Marilee responded, unperturbed. Trent wisely stayed mum, leaving Marilee to handle damage control for her business.

"Oh, right, Stanford Platson." Sandro was quiet for a moment. "You know, he responded to a want ad I put in the Sandalwood Chronicle a few months ago. I was looking for a new controller following Emily's move back to her home town, and he applied for it."

Interesting, thought Marilee. "I assume he didn't get the job." She responded.

"In the end, I hired a controller who recently moved here from Kentucky. Unfortunately for Stanford, she was better qualified, but it was a shame to let him down. He was itching to get out of Sturdy."

"Any idea why?"

"He seemed frustrated in the interview, but he didn't go into any detail about why he wanted to leave there." Sandro turned to check how his booth was coping without him. "Oops, I'd better get back. They're flooded. Can't turn down new business!" he chortled, and headed back quickly to the booth from which they had drifted during their conversation.

By the end of the day, the Green Horizons team was exhausted. Both Trent and Jaz said they did not mind the long day, but Marilee knew the truth. They did not want to let her down. *What a great team*, thought Marilee as they trudged slowly back to her car at eight o'clock, nursing sore backs and blistered feet. It was a sharp contrast to how the day had begun. *What was I thinking? How could I have thought this was a piece of cake? Didn't I learn anything from last year's home show? Tomorrow I'll apologize to Jaz and Trent for having tortured them this way. They may think that those are normal working hours when you take a show, but that's not how I like to operate. That's it,* she resolved firmly, *starting tomorrow, we'll work half-day shifts. This is deadly.*

CHAPTER 8

▼

On Wednesday morning, as Marilee ate breakfast, the local television news reported that the Platson house had been broken into. The story was detailed, yet brief. Someone had broken into a residence on Sycamore Place sometime the previous night, while its residents were out. Marilee was sure it was the Platson home. She recognized the house façade and the front landscaping (of course). Evidently, the house had been ransacked and intruders had overturned furniture, ripped pictures from the walls and emptied drawers in the kitchen and elsewhere. A neighbor had called police when she saw what appeared to be a flashlight moving through the rooms. The homeowner had returned while the police were still on the scene, and was understandably upset. Police were in the process of determining whether anything had been stolen and were canvassing area residents today to find out if anyone else had noticed anything unusual around the time the break-in occurred.

As she rinsed her breakfast dishes and cutlery and placed them on the drip tray, Marilee resolved to pick up a newspaper on the way in to work to see if further details were available. No doubt the burglary would be the talk of the town, especially in light of the recent death of one of the homeowners. It would make for juicy gossip in some circles, Marilee knew.

I wonder why Mrs. Platson's house was broken into? Is it related to poor Stanford's death or was it coincidence that two unfortunate events had happened to the same family in such a short period of time? Did someone target Mrs. Platson after learning that she lived alone in that large house, and knew that she went out for bridge on Tuesday nights? It was a bit much to assume. Under that hypothesis, it would seem that some career criminal had kept Mrs. Platson's house under surveillance to determine her comings and goings in planning this break-in. A bunch of mischievous kids would not go to that effort to break into someone's house. It was odd. On the other hand, Marilee was not prone to believing in coincidences.

On her way to work, she pulled into a strip mall that she knew to have a selection of newspaper boxes. She knew that the major newspapers would not likely carry the story. Burglary had become so commonplace that it was hardly news anymore. *What a sad commentary of today's world,* thought Marilee. She dropped a handful of quarters into the slot, opened the door and withdrew a copy of the local Sandalwood Chronicle. It was only a twice-weekly publication, but, thankfully, one of those days was the mid-week edition.

She climbed back into her SUV without glancing at the paper. She knew if the story had made the midnight printing deadline, it would be there. Local news was always a big deal, and she knew the Chronicle frequently scrambled for stories. Anyway, she wanted to have a steaming cup of coffee in her hand before she took a look for the news story and that would only happen once she arrived at Green Horizons.

As she arrived at the garden center, she could already see that the place was abuzz with gossip and discussion. Any news, however slightly, relating to Stanford Platson, sent the place into a tizzy. Understandably, people were edgy and hoped that the murder would be solved soon without further incident.

She slid from the car, newspaper in hand. Undoubtedly her staff already had a copy. She could see them hunched over the checkout counter, focusing on something she could not see. She presumed it was today's newspaper.

"Good morning, Marilee," Justin said, "Have you seen today's Chronicle?"

"Hi everyone," Marilee responded, joining them. "No, not yet. Which story are you talking about?" she asked, not wanting to jump to conclusions aloud.

Jane said, "It seems that Stanford Platson's house was broken into last night. Isn't that bizarre?"

"Yes, I saw it on the news this morning. It certainly is strange. I bought my own copy so I can take a look at the story. What page is it on?" She got the page number, left the group to their animated discussion. She wanted to think about the story in a quiet place where she could consider its possible connection to Stanford's murder.

She made a beeline for her office, and filled the coffee maker with coffee and water. As she waited she sat down and flipped impatiently to the right page, although she didn't have high hopes of learning anything new. This morning's television news report would have provided the most up-to-date news; the Chronicle would have last night's news, at best. But you never know, perhaps the Chronicle contained aspects of the story that the news channel would not find interesting enough to air.

She waited for the coffee maker to finish. She wasn't *that* anxious that she couldn't wait for a mugful of the rich tonic. *Mmm,* thought Marilee as she took her first sip, *that's always worth waiting for.*

Thus fortified for what lay ahead, Marilee was prepared to direct her attention to the break-in article. She was woefully disappointed. It had held so much promise, considering how her staff had been pouring over it. In fact, the article was barely longer than a bi-line. She sighed. Undaunted, she resolved to glean what she could from the write-up.

All it said was that a Sycamore Place residence had been broken into, that the homeowner was out at the time and that the police were still determining if anything had been stolen.

Yes, it definitely didn't reveal anything more than had been reported this morning. *I wonder if there will be a follow up story in the next edition,* thought Marilee. She chewed the inside of her cheek for a moment, then shook her head. *By Saturday's edition, this will all be old news. So how can I learn more?* She contemplated contacting George Blackwell but opted against it. First of all, she couldn't go around calling police officers to pump them for information. After all, they had a responsibility to maintain confidentiality of such things, and secondly, they were paid to keep the community safe, not stay near the phone so that people could call them for inside gossip. Not only that, George worked in homicide, not burglary. He may not even know any more than she did. Marilee sighed. This was getting harder than anticipated. She paused. Would she be wearing out her welcome if she paid a return visit to the widow Platson? She mulled over the thought in her head. What would her reason be? She couldn't show up again to pay her respects and offer condolences. Hmm, she would have to give that some thought.

Regular business took over her time. One issue arose after another, and Marilee spent the rest of the day putting out fires.

Chapter 9

▼

A few days later, Marilee was operating the checkout. It was an easier job than lifting and moving shrubs and trays of perennial around, but standing on your feet with little opportunity to walk around was tiring and just as tough on one's back and legs. For Marilee, it was an opportunity to rotate through the various roles at the garden center, and it allowed her to see problems she might otherwise never learn about. For some reason, people sometimes became used to working around a problem rather than having it fixed. In one recent example, the till had become sticky and did not open easily when a sale was rung in, so her staff had improvised a solution that involved sliding a ruler under the drawer to force it open. When Marilee found out, she immediately placed a service call to have the drawer adjusted. She would potentially never have found out about the problem if she did not occasionally work the checkout.

Probably what drove the behavior was a wish not to cause aggravation to their boss. Didn't they realize that it was the faulty equipment, and not they, that caused the aggravation? Perhaps he or she did not want to be the one to tell her, in fear of having her irritation rub off on them. Whatever the reason, she hoped her immediate action demonstrated her commitment to providing them with functional equipment, and that they had nothing to fear from her in this regard.

At the moment, thankfully, the cash register was working well. In between customers, Marilee experienced moments of idleness, and helped out with the perennials when she could, always keeping her eye on the checkout. She didn't want any customers kept waiting. That wasn't good for customer relations!

A while later, she headed back to the checkout to ring in a customer's purchase. As she walked around the counter, she recognized Glenda Platson. "This is a surprise, Glenda. We haven't seen you here in some time. What brings you to Green Horizons today?" Marilee smiled at her warmly.

Glenda returned the smile. Marilee noticed that she seemed more together than on their previous encounter. At the same time, it appeared that something was bothering her.

"Hi there, Marilee." She looked at Marilee, embarrassed. "Yes, it's been a few years since I've been here," She looked around. "You've changed a few things, I see." She pointed. "You used to keep the miniature roses over there." She looked over her shoulder, pointing at another spot. "And at one time you sold Koi from raised tubs over there, if I recall correctly." She squinted at Marilee.

Marilee laughed. "Yes, you're right. My goodness, that was a few years ago! I decided to stop selling Koi. We couldn't keep the cranes and herons from considering the tubs their personal feeding stations."

"So how are you, Glenda? I hear you've had another unfortunate incident. A break-in at your house? Are you all right? Was anything of value taken?" Marilee was curious.

At the mention of the break-in, she burst into a stream of frustrated commentary on the event. "You should have seen it! It was awful. I was so heartbroken when I saw the destruction and damage. I now have all sorts of work crews in the house, patching up the holes that were left in the walls when the furniture was tossed around. What a disaster. I don't know what the world is coming to. I can't see any reason why anyone would break into my home. From what I can see, nothing's been taken. I guess I should be grateful that I wasn't home when the burglary happened. The police posted someone to stay with me that night, and the following day they came back to see if anything had been taken. Frankly, it's taken me a few days to put everything back, and when I did, I couldn't find anything missing." She shrugged her shoulders and continued.

"Anyway, I thought I'd come by and replace the houseplants that were destroyed during the break-in. Can you believe it, whoever did it even dumped all the planters upside down, killing the plants and spreading potting soil everywhere. I have no idea why they would do that, yet not take anything." She paused. She leaned forward as if to share a secret. "Not that I keep anything valuable in the house. I'm not much for jewelry, and what I have is kept in a safety deposit box at the bank."

"Anyway," she said looking down at her purchases. "I'm just replacing the plants we had, nothing new. So I'm here to buy a couple of African violets, a palm tree, a crown-of-thorns, and a few ferns and peace lilies." She chuckled. "At least they didn't get away unhurt, though. It looks like the intruder, or one of the intruders, was stabbed by the sharp spines on the crown-of-thorns. Serves them right, too, breaking into someone's house like that." She added gleefully, nodding righteously. "There were a few drops of blood on the plant and on the floor, so the police collected it for DNA testing. They also checked for fingerprints but they won't know if any of them are the intruder's until they've compared them to mine and Stanford's."

"Wow, that sounds promising," replied Marilee as she rang in Glenda's purchases. "I'm glad you weren't home at the time, too. That would have been terrifying! I hope the police are able to catch whoever did it. Did any of your neighbors see anything other than the neighbor who called it in? She has eagle eyes. You must have been very grateful."

"Yes," replied Glenda. "Abby and I have known each other for years. We participate in the neighborhood watch program, in which neighbors keep an eye out for anything suspicious in the area. If you ask me, it just makes good sense to pay attention to what's going on around you and report any vandalism or property damage. Unfortunately, the rest of the people on the street did not report seeing anything out of the ordinary, not even an unfamiliar car parked near my house."

"Who knows, maybe it was just some teenagers looking for a night's amusement after having a couple of drinks too many, in which case they may have just been passing by," ventured Marilee.

"If they come around again, they'll have to deal with me." Retorted Glenda forcefully. "I may not look like much but don't try me when I'm angry!" Flames of fire glinted in her eyes, giving Marilee an inkling of the fury someone could incite if they crossed her.

"Hopefully there won't be a repeat visit to your house. I hope you've made arrangements to install a burglar alarm system since then?" Marilee suggested tentatively. No one wanted further deaths in the community.

"Nah, I'll handle whoever comes my way."

Marilee decided not to press the point. "By the way," she asked, "do the police suspect that this has anything to do with Stanford's murder?"

Glenda looked confused. "Do you think so? No one's mentioned anything like that to me. I certainly hope not. What would they possibly have been looking for?" she looked at Marilee questioningly.

"For one thing, the missing memory card." She assumed that the police had mentioned this to Glenda, and that she wasn't telling tales out of school. She was fairly confident that she wasn't, and assumed the victim's widow would have been the first person they asked about the card. It was a good thing there was no line up behind Glenda, as this conversation was carrying on much longer than a line up permitted, and Marilee was glad for the opportunity to have such a long, uninterrupted conversation with her.

Glenda signed the credit card voucher and grabbed the handle of her cart in readiness to leave. "If it is, I doubt they found it, otherwise the house would have been only half tossed. I doubt it even has any significance. Maybe Stan threw it out because it was defective. Who knows? Anyway, all he ever does with that camera is take flower pictures." She shrugged off the suggestion that there was a possible connection.

Marilee tore off a sheet of plastic liner and walked Glenda to her car, where she helped Glenda place her purchases carefully into the trunk, so they would not fall over during the drive home.

She waved good-bye and headed back to the checkout.

She sure dismissed the burglary/murder/missing memory card connection very quickly. Maybe she doesn't want any further digging into her personal life, thought Marilee recalling her previous conversation with the woman. *But if she accepts the idea that the break-in was perpetrated by someone who was 'passing by', she's kidding herself. No one just 'passes by' a house on a cul-de-sac. Regardless, as far as I'm concerned, she's still a suspect in my books and the break-in does nothing to eliminate her from my list.*

Chapter 10

▼

The following day Marilee made her way to the Sandalwood division of the police department. She checked in with the desk sergeant and asked to speak with Detective Blackwell, giving her name.

Luckily, he was in and within a few minutes he wandered down the narrow dark hallway towards her. He did not look happy.

"Hi, Marilee," he said. "What can I do for you?"

"I just wanted to drop by and see whether there was anything new on the Stanford Platson murder investigation." she said hopefully.

Her inquiry appeared to confirm his suspicions. He took her by the arm and led her outside, where they found a wooden bench and sat down in the warm morning sunshine.

"Are you sticking your nose in again?" asked George. "I told you this was a dangerous case." He slumped his shoulders as if trying to relax. "What do you want?"

"You know, I've been thinking about this case."

"Have you now?" George said sarcastically.

"Yes." Marilee said, ignoring the obvious message in his tone. "And I think there is a connection between Stanford's murder, the burglary and the missing memory card." She paused and looked at him inquisitively to see if he looked surprised or had already made that connection.

His face gave nothing away. "Do you now?"

Okay, now his tone was beginning to irritate her. If he was going to continue making these infuriating remarks, she could see this conversation would go nowhere, but she wasn't ready to leave. She wanted to find out what he knew about the murder, and had hoped it would be easier to pry some small details out of him. It was turning out to be harder than she thought. Damn.

She looked him directly in the eyes. "I bet you've already considered this possibility. Have you?"

George continued to stonewall. "Marilee, you know I can't talk about an open investigation with you. I've already told you more than most people know. And you're pretty smart, too. I have the feeling you have quite a few ideas in that head of yours." He tapped her on the forehead.

She was flattered, but refused to be blocked by his unhelpful commentary. "I hear you were able to obtain DNA, and possibly fingerprints, that were left behind by the burglars, from Mrs. Platson's house."

She looked at him to see if that got a rise out of him.

He sighed. "I imagine Mrs. Platson told you that? I asked her to keep it to herself." He shook his head before looking at her again. "You know, sometimes we have to keep aspects of the crime confidential, so we can ensure that we prosecute the right criminal."

She wasn't falling for that weak line. "But in this case, you don't need that. You will have DNA and maybe even fingerprint evidence with which to nail the perpetrator," she countered.

Damn, the woman was tenacious. "Marilee, there's no proof that the two events are related. You don't know what you're dealing with. Please leave the crime solving to us. We're used to handling dangerous criminals, and we're armed, too." He hoped he had made his point.

The admonishment was old news and did not register with her. Instead, she was frustrated. He was refusing to give her even the teeny, tiniest bit of information. "Okay, at least tell me if any of my employees are still under suspicion. Have they all been cleared off your suspect list?"

George looked her straight in the eye. "Most of them are cleared, but we have yet to confirm alibis for a handful of them."

She looked at him pleadingly. "Can you at least tell me if Pete and Jane have been cleared? I rely on them totally and I would hate to be mistaken about them."

He considered for a moment, and his posture relaxed somewhat. "Okay. Yes, Pete and Jane have been cleared. There. Are you satisfied that you pried something out of me?"

"Yes! Thank you, George," she said, elated. "I'm sorry to have been such a pain."

George smiled. "That's all right, Marilee. I know you're concerned about your staff and your business, and the sooner the killer is caught, the sooner we can all rest easy."

They got up and exchanged good-byes. As Marilee headed to her car, she turned back to watch as George re-entered the building. At least she had learned that he knew 1) about the burglary, and 2) that there might a connection between the murder and the burglary. And she was pleased that at least Pete and Jane were no longer considered suspects. She heaved a relieved sigh.

Chapter 11

The following morning she did not feel nearly as elated. Some uncomfortable thoughts had invaded her mind almost the minute her fingers had turned the car key in the police parking lot the day before.

It seemed odd that several of her staff had not been cleared of the Platson murder. Why was that? Okay, some people were not at Green Horizons that day, so police would have to approach them at their homes, and subsequently confirm their whereabouts at the time of the crime, which would take time. Also, she had to admit; sometimes alibis were hard to come by. Not everyone spent all of their free time in the clear view of others. People could have been home, alone, reading, watching TV, sleeping or playing video games for all she knew, which meant they may not be able to reel off a string of witnesses who could vouch for their whereabouts that unfortunate Saturday morning. Another possible reason was that the police were busy with other things, and had only so many hours a day to devote to chasing down alibis. Okay, she could buy that. She frowned in consternation. Were other Green Horizons employees truly *suspects*?

Now that was a frightening thought. Not only was a killer loose in the community, but that person might also be a Green Horizons employee. No, that can't be, she told herself doubtfully. Surely George would have told her if there was a potentially dangerous killer in their midst. She thought back carefully and repeated the words he had used. 'Yet to confirm airtight alibis for a handful of them' or something to that effect. Okay, so that does not mean one of them is the killer, she tried to convince herself. That only means that the police haven't been able to contact witnesses as to their whereabouts to complete the police records. She felt unconvinced. Damn!

~

Marilee arrived at work in a foul mood. Regardless, she smiled brightly as she encountered her staff on the way to her office. It wasn't their fault that this murder was weighing heavily on her mind and her brain felt like it was about to blow a gasket. Before leaving home she had resolved to give the whole issue a rest for the day and spend the next eight hours thinking of nothing but garden center business. *That should relieve some of the stress,* she thought as she poured her first coffee of the morning and took a long sip.

It wasn't long before the rest of the staff arrived and Marilee made her rounds to say good morning.

She wore her normal outfit: casual tan colored slacks, a long sleeved green button-front flannel cotton shirt, and heavy leather ankle boots that protected her feet from inadvertent injury. She strapped on her utility belt, in which she kept string, price tags, a waterproof marker, a pencil, calculator, paper and a pair of secateurs that she used for snipping stray or dead branches.

In the shrub lots, Jaz, Jane and Justin were already organizing and sorting shrubs and trees for relocation to the correct northern lots. Generally speaking, these plants were organized by broad categories, including: fruit trees, fruit shrubs, evergreens (with various subcategories, such as columnar cedars, globe cedars, pyramid cedars, and the same for other evergreen types), deciduous trees, flowering shrubs, ornamental shrubs, grasses, a special section for native trees and shrubs, and so on.

Jaz looked up and waved Marilee over.

"Hi, Marilee," she greeted, brightly. "Look at these great yews we received yesterday. I love the color. It's such a deep emerald green. Now that's a sign of a healthy plant," she said admiringly. "We're pricing and labeling them, and then I thought we could put them near last year's stock." She mentioned a price and checked with Marilee that it was correct. Marilee nodded, and quickly joined Jane with the pricing and labeling. They worked up a sweat in the sunny day. It was the fourth week of April, and still generally cool, but this day was shaping up to be warmer than expected for this time of year. Thankfully, water was always on hand. Marilee had been adamant that everyone carry water with them wherever they went on the property. It was important to keep hydrated and she didn't want anyone to collapse from heat prostration. She was pleased that everyone seemed to heed her advice.

After lunch the group worked on a shipment of fresh new annuals just received from their local grower.

"Wow! Now these are something to get excited about!" exclaimed Jaz. Justin looked at her strangely. He couldn't get that excited about plants. For him, this was just a way to earn some money to continue his studies in economics, and it always surprised him to see the open excitement register on his colleagues faces when they picked up a new perennial or annual. It seemed like much ado about nothing. He wisely said nothing.

Jane and Marilee looked at the plant Jaz was holding up for admiration. It was a beautiful Gerbera daisy covered in a mass of perfect, bright orange blossoms. The flowers were huge, at least four inches across. Truly, they were a wonderful sight to behold. "I would cover my whole garden in these, if I could," said Jaz. "I can't believe how perfect they look. Honestly, they look almost artificial." She gazed admiringly at the plant.

Jane and Marilee couldn't help but agree. The plant was truly stellar. Marilee sighed. That was the problem with working at a garden center, if you could call it a problem. You wanted to take everything home and plant it in your own garden.

Marilee nodded at Jaz as she put it aside to take home. There was a whole tray of Gerberas, all very beautiful, but that plant was an absolute winner. Marilee hoped that Jaz would enjoy it in her summer garden.

At afternoon break, Marilee headed into her office. A few minutes later, Pete showed up in her doorway, wanting a few minutes of her time.

"Of course," she said, inviting him in to take a seat in one of her guest chairs. "What's the matter?"

"You know that student, Tom, we hired a few weeks ago? He's not doing so well. People are coming to me saying they can't find him half the time. And then I find him somewhere behind the storage huts. Not doing anything, mind you. It's not like he's smoking pot back there, or something like that. He just seems to go off by himself without telling anyone, and we have to go find him. He's a little odd," Pete explained.

"So, have you spoken with him about it? What did he have to say?"

"He apologizes and heads back to work. He seems like a good enough guy but I don't know why he's acting this way."

Marilee considered the situation. Really, they didn't owe Tom anything. He'd barely been working there a month, and if he wasn't working out, they could easily find another student to take his place. Students were always on the look out for well paying summer jobs. "I'm sorry to hear that, Pete. It would be a shame to lose a trained employee." She paused. "Pete, I think we both know what our options are. Let me take a look in his file to see if I can learn anything that might be helpful, and we'll get together to review the situation again at the end of the day."

Pete agreed and sauntered out. As far as he was concerned, Tom could pack up his stuff and go home. Pete had no time for people who couldn't pull their weight. And, like Marilee said, they could replace him in a flash. On the other hand, if Tom could pull himself together, Pete would have no trouble continuing to work with him, and put all of this behind them. It was time-consuming to train new people, and trained employees were always more valuable than new ones.

Marilee pulled out Tom's employee file. Tom Dearling, was his name. She didn't know what she expected to find in his file. Traditionally, employee files contain only basic employment data, memos confirming promotions, and salary increases, unless the employee had acted irresponsibly at some time in their Green Horizons career, in which case a record of the problem behavior was kept in the employee's file. Sometimes, the files contained a note reminding them not to rehire the student the following year due to disruptive or unproductive performance. That was often the case when the student had not been sufficiently problematic to let go, but sufficiently problematic not to be invited back the following year. Usually, the student problems she had revolved around attendance, and sometimes horseplay with the equipment, for which there was absolutely no tolerance. There was no way that she would let herself be characterized in any way as condoning behavior that would be dangerous or could harm anyone. In Tom's case, Marilee expected that the file was fairly thin, and contain only basic information that he would have been required to provide in order to be added to the payroll after accepting his offer of employment. She was right. There were exactly two pieces of paper in his file. She felt dejected.

She wondered whether they should let Tom go or try to get him to pull up his socks. However, getting difficult behavior corrected usually involved getting to the root of it, and Marilee was no psychologist, nor did she have the time to play babysitter to him. *This is a business, for crying out loud!* Marilee returned Tom Dearling's file to the cabinet and noisily slammed the drawer shut in frustration. She put her head in her hands to massage her forehead. She should not get stressed about these things. It happened every year with one or two new students. With returning students it was less of a risk. They already knew what was expected, so the adjustment time for them to get back up to speed was short. Those that did not enjoy their first season tended not to reapply.

New students sometimes failed to adjust to the environment or the heavy work. It wasn't a cushy office job; that was for certain. Depending on the work you were assigned, you might be using or be surrounded by noisy rock or tree moving equipment. If not, you were lifting and carrying sometimes-heavy plants to and fro. There were few tasks that were performed indoors, so most of the time, you were exposed to the elements, which could include very cold periods in the spring and fall, rain throughout the year, glaring hot sun in the summer, and sometimes (very rarely) freak hail or snow storms. And the wind. A constant breeze blew across the land, and even the covered annuals section was open to the wind, so unless you were working in the office area, you were subject to the wind wherever you were. The wind blowing from the south produced a fine layer of sand that coated their hair and clothes daily.

So was that it? Did Tom have an issue with the heavy work or being constantly subject to the cold, wind and rain? Marilee thought not. If Tom had an issue with these things, he would not disappear behind the utility buildings. That might protect him from the wind, but not from the cold. Anyway, the days were warming up now, and a good fleece, wool or cotton sweater topped by a rainproof windbreaker could ward of any chill at this time of the year.

Marilee sighed and resolved to speak with Tom at some point in the afternoon to see what was bothering him. She owed him that much, at least. He was a lot less difficult than most employees. He was quiet, and didn't complain about his shifts or his pay rate, and didn't play around with the equipment for his own amusement, which was important. Perhaps the issue was simple and could be resolved through a brief conversation. Marilee hoped so.

She looked at the time, stood up from her desk and headed for the lunchroom. Maybe she'd be lucky and catch Tom there taking a break. She was wrong. She grabbed a pop, inserting a few coins into the slot before keying her selection.

With pop in hand she headed out to the field where Pete had told her Tom was working today, which was the south deciduous tree lot. She slid her cap's visor back on her forehead to see if she could recognize him from the handful of helpers working the lot today. When she couldn't recognize Tom, she took a chance and headed to the Quonset hut that housed the large moving equipment. It was worth a shot. Contrary to traditional Quonset huts, many modern huts were more cost-effectively constructed, and consisted only of a number of aluminum ribs over which durable white plastic sheeting was stretched. Despite this construction, they were actually quite large, about thirty feet long and fifteen feet high in the middle, with framed doorways at both ends. It was in these huts that the less valuable items, trees, fertilizer, soil and other greenery, were kept. For the large equipment, a tradition Quonset was used. It was similar in design: it consisted of aluminum ribbing, but instead of sturdy plastic, it was covered in corrugated aluminum sheeting.

On her right, Marilee passed one of the newer style of hut. It was filled with manure, topsoil and loam, as well as overstock garden tool inventory. She continued on to the large equipment hut, and kept walking until she reached the back. As she rounded the corner, she hoped he would be there. It would be a lot easier to speak with him here, where he seemed to feel comfortable and they would not be overheard. A disciplinary conversation was a private matter, and Marilee's experience told her that it should be conducted in a one on one setting.

Thankfully, Marilee was right. Tom was there.

"Hi there." She said casually.

It was a moment before he could speak. She could tell that he was surprised and taken aback that she had found him in his hiding spot. "Hi," he managed.

Marilee took a moment to study him. He had a narrow, bony stature, with nearly black hair dangling from the edges of his baseball cap. His face was rather plain. The only notable feature was his dark eyes lined by thick, straight lashes. He was still suffering from teenage acne, which probably caused him some embarrassment and was likely partly to blame for his quiet demeanor. He seemed to be about five foot eight, which was about average for his nineteen years.

Marilee could feel him studying her as well. She hadn't said very much to him since his summer job had started and it was his first close-up look at his boss.

Marilee smiled to herself. She wasn't used to being scrutinized in this way, but it didn't faze her. When she felt he had finished his assessment, she opened the pop and handed it to him.

"How's it going, Tom?"

Again he reacted. She guessed he didn't think she had remembered his name, and it was probably his first inkling that the encounter was not coincidental, which, unfortunately, did nothing to put him at ease.

"Okay."

"How do you like your job so far? You've been here what, three weeks?"

Tom nodded. "It's okay." Tom was turning out to be a man of few words. *Hmm,* thought Marilee, *I hope this isn't going to be more difficult that I thought it would be.*

She tried again. "So what are you working on today?"

"We're moving some trees around. Pete said we have to move the trees that were two years old last year, to the three year old tree lot, and re-price them."

"I see. And how to you like that?"

"It's fine." He drew lines in the ground with a stick.

"What job did you have last summer?"

"I worked at Burger King."

"Huh. And how do you like working here compared to working there?"

"I like this better. I'm getting a dollar an hour more than I was making there!"

Gosh, she thought, *how flattering. Was that the only positive aspect of working at Green Horizons that he could think of?* Subliminally she shook her head to get back on track. This topic wasn't getting her what she wanted. She tried another tack.

"Do you live in Sandalwood, Tom?"

"Yes, my mom and I moved here last fall." He glanced at her cautiously. "I don't have a father. Mom says he left us when I was a baby." He paused, considering how much he wanted to share. "She married when I was five. Barry, my step-father, he was okay, but they got divorced when I was twelve, so since then it's only been us two."

Marilee was silent for a moment. "I see. So have you moved around a lot?"

Tom nodded. "Mom doesn't like her job much, so she is always hoping that she'll get her big break in the next town." He laughed bitterly. "She's a cashier at the Buy and Save." He added.

Marilee waited. It was the longest string of words he'd put together yet, and she hoped that there was more.

Tom continued to scratch in the dirt with his twig. Looking at the ground, he said, "I just wish my dad had come back to us. Then we would have become a real family and Mom and I would have stopped moving around." He glanced at her.

Marilee felt for him. Children needed parental support to feel safe and loved, and it was easier when the family contained two parents. How difficult it must be for Tom's mother to raise him on her own, and deal with her own issues at the same time.

"What are you studying at school?" she asked.

His face lit up. "I'm majoring in Finance, with a minor in Economics."

"Wow, that's impressive. How is it going?"

"I've finished first year. It's going great. I enjoy Finance. Mom says it's because I take after my Dad." A small thought twigged in Marilee's mind, but was gone before she could catch hold of it.

Tom continued. "College has been a big adjustment from high school, but I enjoy the courses, and my grades are pretty good!" It was the first time he'd shown any animation.

"I'm happy to hear that." She paused. "Tom, I'm going to make you a deal." Marilee said, looking him straight in the eye. "You know that everyone needs you to pull your weight around here, right?"

Tom blushed and looked at the ground again. He didn't like where this conversation was going.

Marilee continued. "I would like you to keep this job. I think you are a capable employee, and I believe that you will have a successful finance career in the future. But right now, everyone needs you to do your bit. Everyone is working hard, and we need you to do the same. For my part, I promise to be available if you ever want to talk. About anything at all," she said earnestly. He looked at her. He had understood the references to working and keeping his job, and knew it was a serious conversation they were now having.

"That means, Tom, you can't go sneaking off and hide somewhere. If you need a break, clear it with Pete first, okay? You have probably already figured out that Pete's a pretty reasonable guy. Right?" She gave him a steady look.

Tom nodded. "Okay," he said and stood. He smiled. "I guess this means I'd better get back to work, now." He gulped the last of the pop.

"Here, give me that," Marilee offered, smiling up at him. "I'll put it into the recycling bin."

As they both headed back to the front of the lot, Marilee jabbed him gently on the shoulder, and he laughed as he playfully leaned out to avoid her punch.

Chapter 12

The following day, the mail arrived around 10 o'clock as usual, and Marilee retrieved it from the counter where Jane normally placed it. Not surprisingly, it contained a number of utility, repair and supplier bills as well as the usual unwelcome fliers trying to sell everything from bottled water to dating services to real estate. One letter from the local board of trade caught her eye. Postponing opening the inevitable invoices, she slid her thumb under the flap of the board of trade envelope. She glanced quickly through the contents of the letter and realized it was a reminder for the quarterly gathering of Sandalwood area business owners. As in other towns and cities, the board of trade was an organization that promoted new businesses in the region, and member organizations met periodically to discuss issues of common concern such as property taxes, zoning issues and new competitors planning to move into the area.

The meeting was scheduled for the following evening. Wow, thought Marilee, not much notice, as reminders go. She made a note on her calendar to attend.

Chapter 13

▼

Wednesday came and Marilee left Green Horizons around 5:30 to arrive at the dinner meeting by six o'clock sharp. She hated to be late. For anything. Lateness meant you had to enter a full room after dinner or festivities had begun, which was intimidating, she felt, to probably everyone except a closet performer. No, she preferred arriving early so that she could pick her own seat, and hopefully influence who would join her table.

Because Marilee's business did not permit her to wear 'business' clothes during the day, she had taken the opportunity to change into a delightful deep purple pantsuit with a hot pink sleeveless knit top before leaving work. After freshening her makeup and hair in the women's washroom at Green Horizons, she felt she looked suitably business-like and ready for the meeting.

The drive to the board of trade offices was uneventful, and Marilee's mind wandered. Over the past few days she had given little thought to the Platson murder, and she wondered what progress George had made since the last time they had spoken.

She recalled their last meeting, remembering his unwelcoming tone, and hoped that their next meeting would take place on a better note.

In fact, she herself had made no progress since that conversation. She had intended to have a handle on the motive by now. She frowned, and an enlightening thought occurred to her. Perhaps Charles Kingly of Sturdy Roofing Installations would be at tonight's dinner! That would be a stroke of luck. She spent the rest of her drive determining how to arrange a seat at his table, if he did, in fact, attend.

As she pulled into the parking lot, several business owners had already arrived. *I guess a lot of people had the same idea,* she thought. She only hoped that the event wasn't filling up so quickly that she would not be able to influence the seating arrangements. She hurried inside.

People milled around the bar, purchasing drinks to pass the time until dinner was announced. *Good idea,* thought Marilee, as she ordered a glass of her favorite Chardonnay. She planned to remain alert, and had already decided that one drink would be sufficient this evening.

A group of acquaintances waved her over, and Marilee was soon engaged in entertaining stories and jokes. The time passed quickly and shortly after six o'clock, the membership was invited to seat themselves for dinner. As they entered, the beauty of the room engulfed them. Marilee had attended events at the venue before, but it had never been so magnificently decorated. Tables were decked with a two-layer organza on linen tablecloth, and chairs were similarly adorned. Elegant as it was, the room was overdone for the nature of the event, and Marilee could hear the other attendees murmuring comments as they attempted to detect the reason. Now she felt inadequate although she had felt suitably dressed moments before. She looked at the other attendees to see if she had misinterpreted the event's dress code, although anything more formal would have been out of the ordinary for the usually humble and practical local business owners.

As she scanned the crowd, she saw Charles Kingly, surrounded by a group of loudly chatting men. Marilee excused herself from her companions and approached him. As she attempted to introduce herself, she received a rude elbow to the ribs, and the offender apologized briefly with barely a sideways glance before continuing his discussions.

Determined not to let herself be so quickly derailed, she opted to apply her next best strategy, which was to stay nearby and hope that she would end up at the same table as Charles. It had become impossible to get his attention, and, although the idea was a lame one, she felt it had potential. Her hopes were dashed, however, when his contingent occupied all of the available seats, and Marilee was forced to sit at an adjacent table. The result turned out to be preferable, because she was once again in the company of her earlier acquaintances and would simultaneously be able to keep her eyes and ears on Charles Kingly without raising suspicions.

Serving staff moved silently around the tables, filling water glasses and offering to place napkins on women' laps. A man, evidently a representative of the board of trade, picked up a microphone and spoke to the gathering. As everyone strained to hear, they learned that there had been a mistake with the dinner arrangements and that, at no additional cost, they would be treated to a luscious five course dinner consisting of cold shrimp in a glass served with seafood sauce, mixed salad greens with raspberry dressing, butternut squash soup, roast leg of lamb, braised French potatoes, and seasonal vegetables, followed by a desert of baked Alaska accompanied by coffee and tea, instead of the planned menu. The cheers, whoops and yells drowned out his repeated apology, but no one seemed to care. Everyone was pleased with the surroundings and the succulent dinner awaiting them, and the drinks they had consumed at the bar earlier enhanced their appreciation of the situation.

Having thus been uplifted, everyone chatted easily as the first course arrived.

Marilee learned quickly that she would not have to work very hard to listen in on Charles Kingly's conversations. He was a large, opinionated man, and he did not hesitate to let his deep voice boom above the numerous other conversations taking place in the room. Marilee caught snippets of conversation that predominantly focused on various building projects taking place in the area. It seemed that Charles had a number of lucrative projects on the go. *The roofing business must be thriving,* thought Marilee. *Good for him.*

Once desert and coffee were served, the presentation began. Today's topic was zoning, which was bound to be a contentious issue. A number of business owners were hoping to expand into neighboring properties or had their eye on prime real estate lots, and were barred from carrying out their plans by existing zoning regulations. The board of trade had created a special committee tasked with creating a strategy for working collaboratively with regional town counselors to influence changes to the bylaws and the purpose of today's presentation was for the newly created committee to provide its first update. Marilee hardly listened. She had no interest in moving or expanding her location, and as long as there was no move to rezone her existing premises, she was marginally interested in the proceedings. She had attended to network with community leaders and stay in touch with issues of concern.

Marilee became aware that Charles Kingly's seat was vacant, as were a number of others at his table. *That's odd,* thought Marilee, *when did that happen?* She excused herself quietly and made her way out to the lobby to see if she could spot him. She rummaged through her purse, pretending to look for her cell phone to make a call. She rationalized that it would not be difficult to locate him; his voice and size would betray his whereabouts.

Charles Kingly was nowhere to be seen. Disappointed and surprised that she had lost track of him, she decided to take advantage of the break and headed to the ladies room. As she passed the coatroom, she heard voices. She paused and tried not to make a sound so that she could hear the conversation. *Damn!* Someone had started the hand dryer in the ladies' room and for a moment the words were drowned out. Marilee would have to wait, which she did, patiently.

A woman left the ladies' room, and Marilee resumed her listening. She wasn't gathering much, but she could not be mistaken about Charles Kingly's voice. He was definitely a party to the discussion. Every once in a while the volume of the discussions rose, but the words continued to be unintelligible. Marilee became frustrated. Pretty soon someone would see her, and she wasn't doing a good job of pretending to be either going to the ladies' room or making a phone call. She strained her ears. "… building inspections … come to inspect … be prepared … make sure … " The voices rose and Marilee knew the conversation was about to end. She quickly slipped through the ladies' room door to avoid being caught eavesdropping and made it just in time. She heard the door to the coatroom creak open on poorly lubricated hinges and the men's shoe soles slap the stone floor as they made their way back to the meeting.

Wow! Thought Marilee. *I wonder what that was all about. Too bad I didn't see who Charles was speaking with,* she thought with regret. But she had been smart to leave when she did. Who knows what would have happened if they had caught her listening? She heaved a deep sigh of relief. She felt exhilarated. Was it possible that Platson's murder was linked in some way with building inspections? Marilee could not see how. Platson was not involved in the day-to-day operation of the business, and it was unlikely that he visited work sites, much less attended building inspections. Marilee had to admit she was jumping to conclusions. There wasn't any proof that the conversation she had overheard had anything to do with Platson. Where moments before she had felt elated, she now felt dejected. It was true: it was possible that none of this had anything to do with Platson, and, in fact, she had not overheard anything even remotely illegal. The only thing that had made the conversation seem odd was that it had taken place in the coatroom, but that didn't count for anything.

Chapter 14

Friday began as another beautiful sunny day. The garden center was humming. Glorious days always made for good sales. No one wanted to even think about planting when the weather was cold and nasty.

Marilee returned to her office to refill her coffee cup and headed back outside to take a moment to enjoy the day. Customers were making the best of it, and the selection of plants was at its peak. In the garden center, petunias, African daisies, begonias and impatiens were overflowing the benches. For those who liked to create their own hanging baskets, an abundant supply of trailing annuals burst from their tiny cell packs. White-flowering pacopa, green or eggplant colored potato vine, asparagus fern and seed geraniums were some of the favorites for hanging baskets.

On the perennial tables, some plants were in full bloom. There, an array of rose-colored perennial bleeding heart, white Dutchman's-Breeches, pink wispy gaura, purple peach-leaved bellflowers, pale pink musk mallow, assorted calla lilies, liatris and lavender colored Russian sage flowered in a bewildering mixture of scents and shades.

As she watched the shoppers roaming the aisles with their carts and flat-bed trolleys, she realized another good thing about running a garden center: the customers were always happy. Okay, every once in a while you were faced with a grumpy customer, unhappy that a plant had not made it through the winter, or complaining that some aspect of a landscaping project that had not turned out as expected. But overall, they were a contented lot, she thought as she leaned against a pillar inhaling the intoxicating, fresh coffee scent as she gazed across the perennial and shrub lots.

~

Later that afternoon, Marilee and Justin drove to the Buy and Save for some supplies for the following day's customer barbeque. The Buy and Save was a few miles down the road from Green Horizons and they arrived within a few minutes.

Marilee asked Justin to grab a cart and fill it with a selection of pop while she went on the hunt for hot dogs, hamburgers, buns, condiments, napkins and plastic cutlery, as well as to get some ideas on desert.

Half an hour later, they met, laughing, at the checkout counter. Both of their carts were overflowing, and Marilee wondered if they would have enough room in her SUV.

They lined up at the cash register, and waited, discussing tomorrow's event and how to organize it. Soon it was their turn. As the purchases were rung in, Justin made himself useful by bagging the groceries, letting the cashier focus on scanning the seemingly endless mound.

Marilee handed him the keys and Justin headed out to start loading the truck as she paid for the purchases. For the first time, she glanced at the cashier. She looked familiar, somehow, but Marilee was sure they had not met before.

"Hi, I'm Marilee Bright. You must be new. I usually recognize the cashiers."

The woman at the register glanced at Marilee and said, "I've only been in town since last year. I'm Diedre Dearling."

The name registered. "You must be Tom's mother."

Now she could see the resemblance. They shared the same straight, narrow nose, thin, pale mouth and angular jaw, but that's where the similarities ended. Where Tom had dark eyes, she had pale green ones, flecked with hazel, and where he was tall, she couldn't have been much more than five foot four inches tall. A thin ponytail captured her mousy, dark blonde hair. A wrinkled brow completed the picture, as if she was perpetually concerned. Marilee guessed that she was about forty years old, but looked several years older.

The woman looked at her suspiciously as she brushed a lose strand behind her ear. "That's right. How do you know that?"

"Sorry, I should explain. I run Green Horizons, where Tom's working this summer. I thought I recognized something familiar about your face. Now I know what it is. He has the same nose and mouth as you do."

Diedre's face relaxed. She chuckled. "Yes, I'm glad he took on some of my looks. He's inherited some from his father, too." Suddenly she looked like she wished she hadn't mentioned him. "Tom tells me it's a great place to work," she continued quickly. "He's made some friends there, and he likes the pay, which will come in handy when he goes back to school in the fall. I haven't seen your place myself. Maybe sometime I'll come and take a look at where my boy is working." She said.

"Yes, that would be wonderful." Taking advantage of the reference to Tom's father, and not wanting to let it slip away, Marilee continued. "Too bad about his father, though. I think Tom would have loved to have him around. Do you have any idea where he went? Where does he live?"

Now Diedre gave her a strange look. "His father was Stanford Platson, didn't he tell you?"

~

What?!? thought Marilee as they drove back to Green Horizons in silence. She was glad that Justin had not been in earshot for the conversation, and still she couldn't believe what she had just heard. It was unfathomable. Diedre's comment implied that Tom had known all along who his father was, and hadn't said anything, even when the topic came up in discussion with Marilee. Her emotions were in turmoil. On the one hand she felt stunned and shocked by the revelation. On the other hand, she felt angry with Tom for not being forthright with her, in what she had felt had been an honest conversation.

This is not a good sign, Marilee brooded. The fact that Tom had so easily deceived her was problematic. It meant that his skill at deceiving people was well practiced, and it had implications for the murder of his father.

She shook her head. Unbelievable. She wondered if Tom had shared this important tidbit with the detectives. Clearly, it was a significant piece of information that could very well have a bearing on the police's investigation into Stanford Platson's death.

She thought back to the morning Platson was killed. Where had Tom been at the time? She could not recall. Was he at work that day, or was it one of his days off? She would have to check her records. It wasn't ringing any bells. As it was, her brain was so muddied with this new revelation that she could hardly think straight. She resolved to call George the minute they got back to Green Horizons.

She turned her attention to Justin, who must have wondered what had happened to make her so quiet, and talked of tomorrow's plans on the drive back.

~

On their arrival, Marilee assigned Justin and Jaz the task of storing the supplies, while she walked to her office to call George Blackwell before she did something rash like yank Tom into her office to give him a piece of her mind.

First, she checked Tom's timesheet for the Monday Platson was killed. His time card indicated that he had punched in at 9:57 AM, and suddenly she recalled the morning's events clearly. Tom had arrived late for work claiming car trouble. The garden center had opened, as usual, at nine o'clock and, Jaz had discovered Platson's body sometime within the next half hour. Marilee covered her open mouth with her hand, aghast. That meant that Tom had a clear window of opportunity to kill his father before showing up for work. All he had to do was park his car in a hidden location nearby, commit the crime, return to his car and complete his drive to work. It worked, provided he had not become covered in blood. Alternatively, he could have had an extra set of clothes in the car.

A chill ran down Marilee's spine. Now she was glad she hadn't rushed to call Tom into her office. She recalled the warning George had given her. The killer was intent on remaining anonymous and would likely not hesitate to kill again. She did not want to picture Tom as a killer, but she had no evidence to the contrary. In fact, two things were now pointing in his direction: his late arrival that day, and his failure to disclose that Stanford Platson was his biological father.

This was definitely important enough to call George about. It was imperative that she ensured that he knew about the genetic connection between Platson and Dearling.

She closed the door and took a moment to consider the call before dialing. She remembered her last ill-fated conversation with George. This time she was sure she was not overstepping her bounds. It was important information, and if she did not tell George, he could accuse her of withholding information vital to the resolution of this crime.

She retrieved his number from her contact list and dialed the number.

"George Blackwell, Police Department, Sandalwood Division." he answered mechanically.

"George," Marilee said breathlessly, "I'm so glad I reached you. It's Marilee."

"Marilee, are you okay? You sound frightened. What's going on?"

"I just learned that Stanford Platson was Tom Dearling's father. And Tom showed up late for work the day his father was killed, so he actually had a window of time in which to kill him. My God, George, do you think he's the killer?" she asked in a whisper.

George was thoughtful. "How did you learn about this?"

"I ran into his mother at the Buy and Save. She's a cashier there, and she mentioned it to me. It was big news to me, considering I've had a few conversations with Tom, and he never said a word."

"I see. It's news to me, too. You're right, Marilee, this is very important information and definitely has a bearing on this investigation. Meeting the father who abandoned you could cause some strong feelings, and that could easily have driven Tom to commit this crime, especially if his father rejected him when Tom disclosed his identity, if he did." He paused and she could tell he had placed his hand over the mouthpiece to speak to someone in his office. "Okay, Marilee. Jim and

I are heading over there right now. It will take us about 20 minutes. Will Tom still be on his shift, or will he be finished for the day?"

Marilee checked the time on the phone. "He will be finished in about half an hour. If you haven't shown up by the time he's ready to leave, I'll delay him for you."

"Thanks, Marilee. That would be helpful." He hung up.

Marilee sighed. She was exhausted. This situation had pumped adrenaline through her body and now she was starting to feel the aftereffects. Thankfully, George and Jim would arrive soon to take charge of the situation. If Tom was the killer, she hoped they arrested him on the spot thus relieving everyone's worries.

She stepped out of her office and headed towards the mature tree lot where she knew Pete and Tom were working today. She caught Pete's eye and hailed him. He was operating one of the heavy lifting trucks, moving landscaping rockery. He cut the engine and stepped down from the cab before heading towards her.

She pulled him aside. "Pete, the police will be here shortly to re-interview Tom," she started seriously. "Can you please help me keep an eye on him until they arrive? Don't let him leave." Unfazed, Pete nodded, taking in the severity of the situation. "No problem, Marilee." He took a look around for Tom, noted where he was and what he was wearing and vowed to keep him in his sights until the police arrived.

When George and Jim arrived, they collected Tom from the south lots and took him into the lunchroom to quiz him. The door closed quietly behind them. Pete and Marilee sat nailed to their office chairs, nervously awaiting the results of the police's inquiries.

Eventually, the door opened and the three men appeared. George made his way to Marilee's office. In the background, Pete and Marilee could see Jim lead Tom Dearling to a waiting cruiser.

They glanced expectantly at George.

"We have spoken with Tom Dearling. He has admitted to knowing that Stanford Platson was his father. He has also been unable to provide anyone to corroborate his whereabouts at the time of the murder. He says he had a flat tire on the road on the way here that morning, but we have found no evidence to support that story. Based on these two factors, we are taking him down to the police station for further questioning, where we may hold him indefinitely."

Marilee exhaled loudly. "Thank you, George."

"To be clear, Marilee, Pete, he has not been charged with any crime. That means that at the end of our inquiries he may go free." He looked at them to determine whether they had understood. "He may not have killed Stanford Platson. All we have at the moment is circumstantial evidence," he clarified.

Pete and Marilee looked at each other. They had hoped this was the end of it, but it appeared that they would not be so fortunate.

"Okay, we understand," George said. "Thanks again."

After the detective had left, Marilee contemplated what had happened. Studying her fingernails, she said, "I guess that means that, in the short term, we need to decide whether we need someone to fill in for Tom. I'll leave that for you to decide." She looked at Pete. "The more important matter is that we, and by that I mean I, may have been jumping to conclusions about Tom, in which case he'll be back to work in a few days, and we'll have to go on as if he had nothing to do with it." She glanced at Pete to see if she could sense what he was thinking. She couldn't. "What are you thinking about, Pete?"

"I've been thinking about what George said. I agree with you. I really thought that Tom was the killer, and now I see that it could still have been someone else. Just because he was late for work, and didn't tell us he was Platson's son does not mean that he killed Platson." He continued. "So, I will be okay with whatever the police decide. If they keep him in police custody, that's fine. If they release him, I'll take that to mean Tom didn't do it, in which case I'm fine with that, too."

Leave it to Pete to wrap everything up in a nutshell.

"Well," Marilee said, placing her hands on her armrests and pushing herself out of her chair, "I guess that's that. We'll see what tomorrow brings. In the interim, do you need someone to help with the tree lots and rockery, or do you have enough staff to carry on?" she asked, getting back to business.

"You know, I think we'll be fine. Tomorrow I'll tell my staff that Tom will not be back for now. If I find that we fall behind, I'll let you know, Marilee." He nodded. "Good night. See you tomorrow." He headed towards the south lot where he kept his truck.

'Good night' was right, thought Marilee. It's been a long day.

Chapter 15

The following days passed quietly at the garden center. As some of the employees had been around when Tom was arrested, gossip made its rounds and eventually everyone knew. Whispered conversations abounded as people went about their daily work.

The days were getting warmer, and the staff was beginning to really enjoy them. Each year, only a limited period existed where the weather was not too cool and not too hot. In a few weeks they would experience searing heat, so the intervening warm days were greatly appreciated.

Business, also, continued swimmingly. Many of Green Horizons' repeat customers had made their first visits of the season, and had provided amusing anecdotes about the events of the past six months.

Perennials and shrubs continued their wave of blooms. Although forced into an early bloom cycle by the growers, many perennials bloomed again when the weather signaled their normal flowering time.

It was now early May, and hostas had begun to unfurl their large blue-gray and green and white leaves. Ginger plants also spread their hardy, round, disk-like leaves. Silvery lamium leaves reached happily for the sun and pale yellow or pink blossoms appeared on their tiny stalks. Spent blooms from early spring-flowering plants were carefully removed to keep the plants manicured. And always, watering and fertilizing were imperative. No one wanted to see the plants succumb to the drying wind or the beating sun. An occasional rainfall was welcomed, as it provided a respite from the sometimes-manual watering process.

Eventually they learned that Tom Dearling had been released from jail due to lack of evidence. He had been unable to provide names of people who had witnessed his car trouble, and refused to provide a DNA sample. While he did not resign from his job at Green Horizons, he also did not return to work, and Marilee sent his employment paperwork to his home to acknowledge that she understood that he had no plans to return. Likely, the prospect of returning to his place of work was too stressful for him, and he did not relish the thought of his coworkers' reactions. He was probably facing similar issues on the street as people avoided him or glanced at him warily. The fact of the matter was that he was the closest they had come to a viable suspect. Because the case was not closed, and he had not been cleared outright, people still saw him as the most likely candidate for the crime and avoided him.

Marilee wondered if Tom would leave town. If ever there was a reason, this was it. Yet, day after day, she heard stories that confirmed he was still in Sandalwood. So-and-so had seen him or his mother at the Buy and Save. He'd been spotted at the local convenience store or ATM.

Chapter 16

▼

Marilee had made dinner arrangements with her friend, Sarah. They agreed to meet at the restaurant at seven o'clock. The restaurant, called 'The Mandolin', was a local Italian eatery and known for its excellent pasta and seafood dishes. Marilee arrived at the stroke of seven, and rather than wait outside and risk having their table given away, she ventured inside and asked to be shown to her table, while advising the maitre d' that she was expecting someone named Sarah to join her.

The maitre d' showed Marilee to a window table at the front of the restaurant, where she sipped water until her friend arrived a few minutes later.

As she headed into the restaurant, Marilee caught her eye and waving her over. They greeted each other joyfully. They had not seen each other in several months.

Sarah worked as a manager in the municipal offices and oversaw the issuance and renewal of business licenses. It was a career she excelled at and her long tenure in the role attested to her affection for the job. She'd worked there for more than twelve years.

After each ordered a glass of merlot, they concentrated on the menu. Marilee decided to go for the seafood lasagna, while Sarah opted for the spaghetti putanesca. "I can't pass up a chance to have pasta with olives and garlic," explained Sarah.

While waiting for their salads, they updated each other on recent happenings in their lives. Since Marilee knew that Sarah was not a big gardener, she did not broach the topic of new plant introductions, but did provide a brief update on how the garden center business was shaping up for the year. She touched on some of the new personalities she'd hired since opening in early April. Sarah updated her on her love life and the men she'd recently dated. None of them was "the one". They also talked about people they knew, and what events were new in their lives: marriages, divorces, new babies, and deaths of friends, neighbors and acquaintances.

After the salad had been consumed (a delightful mesclun mix with grape tomatoes sprinkled with a balsamic/olive oil/mustard dressing), the main dish arrived. They were both ravenous, so they started in enthusiastically, making only appreciative sounds during the otherwise wordless main course.

When they both came up for air, they sighed contentedly.

"Gosh," said Sarah, patting her stomach, "we should do this more often. I could eat like this at least once a week!"

Marilee laughed and wiped some stray tomato sauce from her chin. "My, what are you eating the rest of the week? Sounds like you're subsisting on candy bars and popcorn!"

Sarah laughed too. "Is it that evident? No, seriously, though, this is great. You know I love Italian food, and it's never this good when I make it at home." She acknowledged sadly that her culinary skills were not restaurant quality, ignoring for the moment that she was comparing herself with chefs that had undoubtedly studied the art of cooking for many years.

"Such is life, Sarah. But you have to admit, if people cooked as well as restaurants did, restaurants would not have a very large clientele, would they?"

Sarah had to agree, despite herself.

"Say," she said, "You haven't told me anything about Stanford Platson's murder! That's got to be the biggest news, and you haven't even said a word about it." She adjusted her chair and leaned into the table in preparation for a juicy, intrigue-rich plot to unfold. Marilee did not disappoint.

"Yes, gosh, you're right. I was beginning to forget about it, since there haven't been any recent developments, but I can tell you everything I know so far."

Marilee told her the story, starting from Jaz finding Platson, to the most recent developments with Tom Dearling. Of course, Sarah was already aware of the more prolific details, as some of the story had been reported in the local and national papers, most notably the murder, arrest and subsequent release of the only suspect in the crime.

When Marilee had finished, they were both quiet. It was a sad and disturbing event, and to have it happen in such a small community as Sandalwood, and the fact that the crime was still unsolved, was unnerving. They dreaded having to acknowledge that there was a killer in their midst.

Marilee also told Sarah about her suspicions connecting the Platson home break-in to the murder.

At the mention of Glenda, Sarah voiced her first observations. "I've heard a few rumors about Glenda Platson. I hear she's a changed woman since her husband died. I don't know her personally, but I know some people who have known her for years, and they say she's much more outgoing than she used to be. It seems that her husband's death turned her into a new woman. She has supposedly updated her hairstyle and is wearing make-up, which she never did before. And she's updated her wardrobe. She used to wear old, frumpy clothes, and you never saw her in anything new. Now, it looks like she's bought a whole new set of clothes. I suspect she's also had laser eye surgery to correct her vision, because her glasses are gone."

"That's a big change from when I saw her, from the sounds of it. When she came to the garden center, she was still wearing those worn, washed-out loose clothes that looked like she'd had them for twenty years. I'm glad to hear that she's not closing herself off from the world, as some widows do." responded Marilee.

"Yes, but that's not all. It seems that the reason she's all dolled up is that she's seeing someone she met playing bridge, from what I understand. My neighbor, Beth, tells me that it's sickening the way the two of them carry on when they're playing bridge. Glenda doesn't think anyone notices, but no one can miss her flirting with Jack Talbot."

Marilee frowned. "Who's he?"

"Jack was widowed a few years ago. Guessing, I'd say he's in his early 50s. He's actually very good looking, so it looks like Glenda snagged herself a great guy. He's a sales representative for a wholesale products company. He sells industrial compressors in Westernly. I hear he's originally from Georgia."

At the mention of that state, a light bulb lit up in Marilee's head. "That explains it. When I visited Glenda, she mentioned that she might move out of state, perhaps to Georgia. At the time she implied that it was because her daughter lives there, but this would give her a second reason. That is, if Jack was planning to move back home and had invited her to go with him."

Sarah moved her chair closer, if that was possible. She was beginning to enjoy the conspiratorial nature of their conversation. "Beth didn't mention anything like that, but you never know. If that's the case, Glenda will put her house up for sale, and we'll soon find out if that happens. Beth would tell me. You know, she loves to gossip." Sarah giggled. "I should really discourage her, but sometimes it's interesting. I learn things I would otherwise never hear about."

Marilee agreed. "How else would we find out things happening in our community? It's not printed in the newspapers, and our own lives only touch so many other people's lives. We can't possibly know everything that's going on with everyone else."

Sarah agreed, and was relieved that Marilee didn't view gossip as something that should be avoided. How boring would that be?

"You know what else Beth told me?" said Sarah, lowering her voice. As Marilee appeared to be all ears, she continued. "I hear that the life insurance on Stanford was a million dollars! Geesh, with that amount of money, she can buy ten new wardrobes *and* move to Georgia, even without selling her house!"

"Wow. Do you know if it's been paid out yet?" asked Marilee, intrigued.

"From what I hear, Glenda is expecting the payment any time now." She paused, and looked at the tablecloth. "What I wouldn't give for a million dollars." She gave Marilee a glance. "Can you imagine what I could do with a million dollars?" She sighed. "I would buy an island in the Atlantic, and just stay there. Did you know that you can actually buy islands? I heard that one recently sold for four hundred thousand dollars. With a million dollars, that would leave a lot left over to live comfortably the rest of your life, no problem." She became silent, continuing to daydream.

Marilee had only been half listening to Sarah's fantasies. Her mind had gone back to thinking about Glenda and a possible motive for killing Stanford. She remembered her notepad in her desk drawer at work. 'Life insurance', she recalled, was the first motive she had put on the list. Now she knew the amount of the life insurance payment, and it was sizeable. But what did it all mean?

No one said that a widow couldn't continue with her life. She was not expected to wear black and grieve forever. How long was a reasonable mourning period, anyway? Stanford had been murdered barely a month ago. Surely the mourning period was at least a year? Marilee's lips curled into a small smile. Some people were probably aghast that the new Glenda was all laughter and light, enjoying her newfound freedom. Anyway, tradition was out the window. These days, people did what they wanted, and did not look to etiquette or protocol to dictate how to behave.

She shook her head, freeing herself from her reverie. Sarah was talking, and she'd missed quite a bit, she feared.

"…to stay in touch with Beth, to find out anything new on the Glenda front," she was saying.

"Yes, that's a good idea," agreed Marilee.

"So are you planning to solve this murder, Marilee? Remember when you solved that book case a few years ago?" Everyone seemed to remember that, thought Marilee. Chuckling, she noted that Sarah had not noticed her own pun.

"Yes, that was fun. But George Blackwell has warned me specifically not to meddle in this. He says it's dangerous, and of course he's right." Marilee propped her head in her hands. "Still, it would be fun to solve. I can only foresee a handful of suspects and motives."

"Do tell." Sarah said excitedly. "What theories do you have about Stanford's death?" She clearly relished the idea of solving the crime. To her, it was like reading a good psychological thriller.

"My first theory is that the crime was about money. Until you said it just now, I had no idea how much Glenda stood to gain from her husband's death. It turns out to be a substantial amount. Like you said, one could buy an island with it. In her case, she'll be able to live whatever life she chooses, even if she only lives off the interest."

"A second theory is that the crime was committed out of anger. Stanford did something unforgivable, and he or she killed him. My suspicion is that Tom learned that Stanford was his father when he and Diedre moved to Sandalwood. Tom approached Stanford to acknowledge him as his illegitimate son. When Stanford refused, Tom killed him in a fit of rage." Marilee paused as though struck by lightning.

"My God, I just thought of something else! What if Diedre killed Stanford? Maybe what happened is that she asked for financial support to help pay for Tom's education, which Stanford refused. She decided that she might have a good chance of petitioning Stanford's estate or the insurance payout on behalf of his illegitimate son if Stanford died!" Now that she had said it, it seemed a bit far-fetched.

Sarah appeared not to have noticed, because she said, "Yes, Marilee, and again, those motives are about money, the same reason why you suspect Glenda. Yikes, there are certainly a number of potential suspects."

"Yes, and there are more. I hadn't finished my list when I thought of that. My other theory is that the crime is business related, and so potential suspects would include someone from Sturdy Roofing Installation and other business acquaintances. This theory is a little more tenuous, as I really have nothing to base it on. The only suspicious thing was that Charles Kingly was acting oddly at the board of trade dinner. I didn't tell you, did I?" when Sarah shook her head, Marilee continued, "Yes, I heard Charles Kingly speaking with someone in the *coatroom* about building inspections. How strange is that?" she asked rhetorically.

Sarah shook her head. "That does not sound good. I am shocked to hear that anyone would interfere with the building inspection system. That system ensures that only safe residential, industrial and commercial buildings are approved for occupancy. I sure hope Charles Kingly is not messing with the inspections. That could have grave repercussions. For example, a factory or reception hall could collapse, killing hundreds of people. Do you have any proof?" She became serious.

Marilee shook her head. "I've tried to put myself in situations where I run into him, but, frankly, I'm limited in the ways I can legitimately be in his vicinity without him getting suspicious. Before I know it, I'll have Charles accusing me of harassment, and George Blackwell will be on my case. I'm in enough trouble with him as it is."

"Hmm, I see what you mean. I might have some better luck." Marilee looked at her hopefully. Sarah had a mischievous glint in her eye. "I can take a look at all of the building permits that list him as the roofer of record. Maybe something will come to light that shows that something strange is going on." She shrugged. "It's worth a try, anyway."

Marilee agreed. It was definitely worth a try, because she had become stymied on this front.

"Any more theories on your list?"

"No, that's it. It's always possible that it was a random act, but based on George Blackwell's experience and his analysis of the crime, he considers that alternative implausible." She became dejected.

"No need to get all depressed, now, Marilee! I just offered to help you. I would think you would be happy about that. We might be able to breathe some life back into your investigation!" said Sarah lightly. The truth was, she was tickled to be able to play a small part in the search for the killer.

Changing subjects, she said, "So, what's on the desert menu? I'm dying for some chocolate!" They both laughed. As if their stomachs weren't full to bursting. But they knew they would make room for desert, and they each ordered something decadent, accompanied by a cappuccino with a shot of Frangelico, to top off their conspiratorial evening.

Chapter 17

▼

There's a proverb that states that people who work in a profession often portray the worst example of their work at home. For example, as they saying goes, a mechanic's car is often notoriously under-maintained because he spends all of his time and effort fixing other people's cars.

Marilee did not reflect this old adage. While not nearly as stellar as the Platson's property, Marilee's gardens reflected her unique taste and style. Her theory was that gardens should be welcoming, relaxing and calming, which precluded therefore any formal plants (topiaries, for one, and rose standards for another). Her preference was for loose flowing plants that did not require trimming and swayed in whichever direction the wind blew them. Despite surrounding chain-link fencing that had been installed by a previous owner, Marilee did her best to create an oasis that, for the most part, screened the fence from her view. White cedars and Austrian pines lined this private place and provided Marilee with a peaceful oasis, away from the public, where she could spend time reading or planting colorful new additions.

It was one of the rare days off that Marilee permitted herself every spring to evaluate her garden and perform much-needed garden cleanup. Black-eyed Susan flower heads had been left for the gold finches to feed on over the winter, and tall grasses had remained to provide a point of interest as they turned from green to rust to gold in the fall, glowing in the sunlight and poking through high snow drifts over the dreary winter days. It was now time to trim them back to the ground to permit new growth to develop, starting the plant's life cycle anew.

She took a deep breath, sucking in the fresh spring air. The morning was perfect for garden work, not too cool, not too warm. Chickadees, robins and mourning doves chirped and cooed overhead, filling the yard with the sounds of nature. *Ah,* she thought as she exhaled the invigorating air and listened to the bird songs, *this is heaven.* She stretched freely in the calm atmosphere, then got to work.

She trod carefully through the garden to avoid crushing the tender tips of emerging hostas and the garden's new growth, snipping off dead leaves, flower stalks and grasses. As gardening went, she found the spring cleanup to be the most time-consuming part, as the garden was, for the most part, self-sufficient, consisting of shrubs, perennials and self-sowing annuals as it did. She had the option of completing the clean-up in the fall, and to some extent she did, but she couldn't see herself going out there on a cold and blustery October day to chop away the still-living leaves of the year's perennials and pick up fallen tree leaves. She invariable missed the last warm, fall day in hopes that there would be more. No, a beautiful spring day was a much better choice she thought.

She was for the most part, pleased with what she had created. Although there were times she admitted that annuals would add a welcome splash of color whenever she experienced a lull in the perennial blooming cycle, she had always felt that planting masses of annuals every year was a redundantly laborious task.

The garden had a number of diverse areas and permitted Marilee the freedom to experiment with any number of sun or shade or dry/moist soil loving plants. Hostas abounded. They were one of her favorite plants, despite the fact that they were predominantly known as ground covers and bore insignificant flowers. It didn't matter. She loved the blue-gray leaves of the shade loving hostas, especially the Siebold hosta, with its large, cup-shaped, puckered leaves, that captured water for the birds as a makeshift birdbath. She also enjoyed the bright, glossy green leaves of the sun-loving varieties, some of which were edged with white. They were also notoriously easy to maintain, although prone to slugs. Another favorite was coral bells. These delightful, scalloped mounts of green, burgundy, yellow or rust leaves produced delicate, wiry stems of small red flowers, aptly named bells, throughout the summer. Foamflowers, a spring-flowering perennial that was similar to coral-bells, grew in pockets throughout the garden.

Some spring-flowering perennials were already in full bloom. Carpets of white, pink and lavender moss pinks and rock cress provided bright spots of color in the otherwise barely waking yard. A few hardy pansies had poked their velvety yellow and dusky black faces into the sunshine. Some had self-seeded in the lawn. Marilee didn't mind a bit. It gave the yard a whimsical, uncontrolled feeling: that the garden should be enjoyed and was not intended to be a formal, stiff place of regimented beauty.

Yesterday she had picked up a few new plants—five each of Stokes' Aster, delphinium, Checkerbloom, Jacob's Ladder, flax—and was eying the various spaces in her yard in which to plant them. Sometimes she agonized over these decisions much more than necessary. She wanted to take into account not only the plant's sun/shade and soil preferences but also her ideas about which color and height combinations would create the most fabulous view. She laughed at herself. Just like the thousands of other perennial gardeners, she had decided early in the spring that her garden was far too bare and needed some filling in, a perception that would not be born out later in the season. And the risk was that one planted the new plants too close to the existing ones, having forgotten their mature size. No problem, she would work it out, or give any leftover plants to an appreciative neighbor.

Her customary tool belt hung loosely from her waist. planting materials were set out: triple mix soil, watering can containing fertilized water, gloves, kneeling pad and shovel. She had also brought a lovely white-blooming serviceberry, and she knew the perfect placement for it. *Right,* she said to herself, *time to get cracking.*

The delphiniums were the first to be planted. She had selected plants of varying hues—purples, blues, white—that she would plant together to produce a breathtaking mass of blooms in early summer.

Unfortunately, she would probably not see blooms this year as the plants required a year to become established and would focus their early energies on building a healthy root system to carry them through the bitter winter before flowering the following season.

She knelt and dug a number of separate holes, each twice as large as the container, to ensure that the plants would have plenty of loose soil to thrust their tender roots into. She brushed a gloved hand across her cheek, and as she did so, she heard a sound behind her. She turned to see a woman opening the side gate to make her way into the yard. Marilee stood. Who would feel so comfortable as to just walk into her backyard without an invitation?

It was Glenda Platson.

"Hi," said Marilee.

"Hi, sorry to barge in like this. I rang the doorbell a few times before it dawned on me that I might find you back here." She looked at Marilee sheepishly. "I hope you don't mind."

"Oh." Marilee paused. "How did you know where to find me?"

"When I was told at Green Horizons that you were off today, I took it upon myself to look you up in the phone book. Your address is listed, you know."

"That's true." Marilee eyed her curiously. "It's unusual for people to go to the effort of looking for me at home. So, what brings you to visit?" She removed her gardening gloves and led Glenda towards a small black wrought-iron table and cushioned chairs.

It was Marilee's first opportunity to look at her fully. Sarah was right; the woman had changed significantly. Not only was her wardrobe upgraded, her bearing was more erect, poised. Today she wore a slim, fitted, sleeveless fuchsia dress, with a cream sweater thrown over her shoulders, buttoned at the neck, together with cream pumps. Without glasses, her face took on an entirely different appearance, more open and welcoming, showing her high cheekbones. She had clearly made an effort to apply makeup in a flattering yet natural manner. Marilee was surprised. For a woman who appeared never to have used makeup in the past, she had done an admirable job. She's had a lesson at the cosmetics counter, she thought.

All of which would have had a better effect if Glenda had not been clearly upset. She twisted a tissue in her hands before looking up at

Marilee. "You asked me before about the memory card from Stanford's camera."

"Yes. I mentioned that the camera was missing a memory card when the police found his, umm, body." She said, trying to be diplomatic.

Glenda appeared not to notice, and continued. "Yes. Since you mentioned that, I've been wondering about it. It's true that it could be connected to the break-in at our, I mean, my house a few days after his murder." She paused and looked at Marilee questioningly.

"That is what I had suggested." Marilee continued, hoping for more information to be forthcoming.

"Yes," Glenda latched onto Marilee's words. "I'm concerned. It appears to me that whoever ransacked my house didn't find the memory card, as I mentioned to you at the time. But what if they come back to look for it again?" A furrow of concern crossed her brow. "And what if there's something really serious on the memory card? If they think I know what it is, I'm afraid..." she trailed off, not wanting to speak the thoughts crossing her mind.

"I see what you're saying, Glenda." Marilee leaned over to pat her hand. "So what do you mean by 'serious'?" Do you know what's on the card?"

"No, I don't." She shook her head adamantly.

"Okay. Tell me, do you know where the memory card might be? Everyone, the police, me, now you, are wondering what happened to that card." She studied Glenda carefully to determine whether she was telling the truth when she next spoke.

"Really, I have no idea. He must have had it with him when he left the house. He would have made sure that the camera had a memory card with space on it. It's like a film camera. You make sure you have blank film in it before using it." She shook her head. "But what if someone thinks I have it, or thinks I know what's on it?"

"I would think that that idea had already occurred to the burglar before he broke into your house. He would have picked a time when you were at home, to get the information or card from you." Glenda shivered at the thought of it. Marilee was trying to comfort Glenda, but realized her reasoning might be faulty, putting Glenda at risk.

"Not to alarm you, but you might be right. The burglar might also have planned to break in the first time to check whether he could find the card himself, with the intent to return at a later date if it became necessary to get it from you. That way, he could avoid violence and running the risk of being identified, and only risk it if he found that step necessary. Sorry, but that is a possibility, too, Glenda, like you said." Glenda looked at her fearfully, with tears forming in her eyes.

"So what should I do?" Her voice cracked with alarm.

"First, I suggest we call Detective Blackwell to let him know of this possibility. Perhaps he will be able to assign officers to guard your home. Second, I strongly recommend that you install a security system. That will make you feel a lot safer. Even if Detective Blackwell can assign some officers to watch your house, that won't go on forever, and you'll want protection after the surveillance ends."

Glenda nodded. "You're right. I know you mentioned that before, but I really didn't take you seriously."

"If you don't mind me asking, Glenda, what changed your mind? Did something happen to frighten you?"

Glenda nodded. "Yes, a few times over the last couple of weeks, I heard strange noises. I ran to my bedroom closet with a baseball bat once or twice, but nothing happened. But that was enough to get me scared." She swallowed. "It sure feels different without Stan."

Marilee nodded in acknowledgment. She knew the feeling. It was always more comforting when someone else was around.

"That's another idea. Do you have anyone who can stay with you for a couple of weeks, until things are resolved? Preferably someone who owns a Doberman." Marilee asked, although joking about the Doberman. Glenda smiled, and it was good to see she still had a sense of humor.

"Yes, I guess I could ask Abby to stay with me." She said, referring to the neighbor who had originally called in the burglary. "She's an interesting personality, and we'd have a great time if I can convince her to do it." She laughed. "She could bring her Cockapoo. He's no Doberman, but he would do enough yelping to frighten off an intruder. Yes, having Abby stay over for a few days would be fun." She smiled, comforted, at Marilee. "That makes me feel better already. Thanks, Marilee."

"I also recommend that you take a look at Stan's computer to see if you can locate any pictures in which he captured something that someone would not like to have known. It could be anything: drugs, homosexual activity, a violent act. I know you don't think the missing card is at home, but it would be worthwhile to see if it's there. Also take a look at any other memory cards he used. If you could find the memory card and identify what's on it, you might help solve this case."

They stood. Marilee patted Glenda's hand as she led her back to the garden gate.

"It always helps to talk things over with someone who can look at things more objectively," Marilee acknowledged.

Glenda turned to her. "I know you've been talking to people, trying to solve Stan's murder, and I appreciate your help. I haven't heard much from Detective Blackwell. I might as well be dead for the amount of information he shares with me." She snorted. "I'll be lucky if he ever calls me back. I call him several times a day, and he just ignores me." She looked at Marilee. "If you can solve this, I would be very grateful." She turned and opened the black chain-link gate. "I can see myself out. Bye, Marilee." and she gracefully and silently made her way out to the street and her car.

"That woman is an enigma," Marilee said to herself as she slipped on her garden gloves and return to her planting.

~

This is crazy, thought Marilee. As far as she could determine, no progress had been made on the Platson murder case. She was sitting in her kitchen table with a steaming cup of honey and lemon ginseng tea after having finished her planting, cleaned her gardening tools and washed up. She wrapped her weary hands around the china cup and contemplated the stalled case. To her, it was incredible that Stanford Platson's murder remained unsolved. It seemed so straightforward. Platson led a very simple life, with very few interests to occupy him during his off-work hours. What could possibly be so complicated about solving his murder? At the same time, she realized she was being unduly hard on everyone who was working on this case. *What had she herself accomplished?* She asked herself. *Not much,* was the answer.

Again she went over what they knew of Stanford Platson. Killed at Green Horizons, likes gardening, works as a financial controller, married, etc. Really, Marilee established, the only clue they had to go by was the missing memory card. It may not lead anywhere, but at least it was a clue, and apparently an important clue, if you linked it to the break-in at Glenda's house. Of course, the police had a DNA sample, too, but that would only prove valuable once a suspect was identified. Until then, it would remain an untapped resource.

Chapter 18

▼

Marilee had already determined what she would do the moment she arrived at work the following morning. She would look through the shrubs and comb the area in which Stanford had been found to see if she could locate the memory card. Granted, the police would have covered the area thoroughly, and, if the card had landed in a plant pot, the plant may very well have been sold by now, in which case they would never find it unless the lucky shopper turned it in. Regardless, Marilee was optimistic. Since the police had not found it and no one had turned it in, she felt that her chances were pretty good.

She had already had her requisite morning coffee, had checked in with her staff, and wore her standard garden center garb as she headed out to the shrub lots. Although some plants had been moved around—another challenge—there was no mistaking where Stanford's body had been found. It would be a long while before everyone forgot that.

She strode purposefully to the area in which he was found and oriented herself. He had been lying in an east-west orientation, with his head pointing westward. Had Stanford been in the process of checking his memory card when he was attacked? If so, the movement of his body being stabbed might have caused the hand containing the card to fly up, in which case it could have landed anywhere. *Please don't let that be the case,* pleaded Marilee silently. She looked about her. Now that the growing season was well underway, the twiggy forsythia and pussy willows she recalled so vividly from that day had given way to full, green, leafy bushes that gave no sign of their former blooms. Only a few remained unsold. No doubt they would remain until the following spring, as customers usually preferred to purchase plants in bloom. The neighboring plants included lilacs, ninebarks and a variety of gold and green leaved spireas. *Good,* thought Marilee. She was sure that those plants had been placed there in early April and had not been moved since then.

She started rummaging through the bushes. Some were still on pallets, and she had to move several plants to check under the pallets and between the slats. Her plan was to move out in ever larger, concentric circles until she found the card. Or gave up. Or died of exhaustion. After an hour, she paused to straighten her back and take a few swallows of water. She was already working on her third circle, having worked first a ten-foot circle, then expanded to 12 then 14 feet. She had yet to find anything, although she did find several mislaid plant stakes, pens and pricing tags, which she gathered up for later use or throwing out, which was probably the case with the pens.

She continued. She was beginning to think that the police had done an excellent job of checking everywhere, when she saw a glimmer of gold between the stalks of a chokeberry bush. She reached to retrieve it, and pulled out the tiny card. *So this is what's causing all the fuss,* she said. The barely inch wide card was predominantly black, with a number of gold-colored (probably copper) metal slots at one end through which the images were probably transferred electronically from the camera. It was slightly longer than one inch, and not more than a few millimeters thick, she observed, mixing her measurement systems. On the Toshiba manufactured device were written "SD" and "2 GB", to presumably denote "storage device" and "two giga-bites", respectively.

Marilee was thrilled with her find, but did not want to appear prematurely victorious. She walked nonchalantly back to her office, her hand hiding the card, unnoticed by patrons and staff. Once she was alone in her office with the door closed, she let herself feel the excitement that had been mounting in her chest. Truly, this was an exciting development, and she called George Blackwell immediately. When she shared the news, he was justifiably elated and said he would be right over to collect it.

After replacing the handset, Marilee sat staring at the memory card. That such a small item could bring big results overwhelmed her. Alone with the card and her office door closed, it didn't take long for her to realize that she could look at the pictures if she inserted it into her computer. That is, if she had the proper card slot and software. It entered her mind that what she was considering would definitely be a no-no in George's eyes. 'Interfering with evidence,' he would probably call it. *But it doesn't hurt to look at my PC to see if I could look at the card,* she rationalized. She pulled her CPU forward to see where the card could possibly be inserted. It would have to be somewhere on the CPU or the screen. The card's metal end would have to fit into the slot, so she picked it up to take a closer look at its dimensions. About an inch wide by a couple of millimeters thick. Wouldn't it be great if she could be the first to see the pictures? Her heart rate shot up as she contemplated the possibilities. Now she half regretted having called George so quickly. She needed more time! After a few minutes more inspection, she realized it was impossible. She dropped heavily in her chair in disappointment. Her computer lacked the necessary card slot. How frustrating. *Time to upgrade,* she vowed. As she searched through her memory, she realized that it had been at least four years since she had last upgraded her machine. There had been no reason to, until now. She sighed in frustration. Another side of her laughed in spite of herself. It was comical that she was considering upgrading her computer because she was frustrated in her sleuthing efforts, not because of a business need. Now that deserved a chuckle. Even so, there was nothing to do now but to wait for George. *Damn!*

They met in Marilee's office, where Marilee handed the card over unceremoniously, a much smaller act than its significance implied. Marilee tried not to look guilty at having considered looking at the card's contents, and shook off her disappointment at having failed.

"Sorry, I touched it." Marilee said hastily, and not a bit chagrined. "But, honestly, I don't think the killer's fingerprints were on it, because otherwise he would have taken it with him." She hoped George would agree with that logic.

"I think you're right about that," he said abstractly, consumed by the little black card and what it might contain. Marilee sighed audibly with relief. George didn't notice.

"So what's the next step, George?"

"I'll take it to the police station," he said as he gingerly placed it into an evidence bag he retrieved from his right jacket pocket. "There I'll have the crime lab take a look at it microscopically to see if any evidence has been deposited on it before they insert it into the computer and look at the contents." He explained.

"When will you know if there's anything interesting on it? I mean aside from plant pictures." She said, knowing that the police department would skim through those shots rather quickly. She didn't see them as botany enthusiasts. Anyway, there would be pressure to zero in on images that could help solve the crime, and presumably the plant photos would not assist in the investigation. She offered her assistance, just in case. You never knew if they would gloss over some images that would speak volumes to her. Maybe he'd taken tons of pictures of poisonous plants, for example. She shrugged mentally, knowing her mind was wandering into a fantasy world where she was the key to solving this crime. George was speaking.

"I imagine we'll know fairly quickly. It shouldn't be more than a few days. And thanks for your offer, Marilee. If we need any help, we'll be sure to give you a call. In the meantime, please do not mention to anyone that you have found this card." He looked at her sternly. "And I mean *anybody*."

As he was leaving, George shook her hand and made his way out. Marilee took a deep breath. She didn't realize she had been holding her breath in anticipation of George's arrival. Wow. She was so excited. She couldn't wait to hear back. Too bad she couldn't tell anyone, but just the knowledge that she had possibly helped find the killer was glory enough.

~

Sarah checked her watch. 6:15 PM. She had been waiting for her coworkers to leave since five o'clock. She cocked an ear to check for any sign that people were still about. All she could hear was the whoosh of the heating system as it blew noisily from the ceiling vent. She waited another few minutes for it to stop and listened again. Silence. Now was her opportunity. She felt weird. It was not her habit to go snooping around in the office, but she had promised Marilee that she would check out the building permits listing Sturdy Roofing Installations to look for anything odd or improper in the documentation.

Sarah's job involved the issuance of business licenses. Building permits were outside her realm of responsibility. She would have to enter another department. If she were found there after hours, she would have some serious explaining to do. She headed out of her own area and made her way down the corridor where she knew the building permits department was located. She passed it every day to reach her own work area. Her palms were sweating, and she hadn't even done anything.

She reached the department, listening at the door and wiping her sweaty hands on her pants before turning the knob and entering. The area was an exact reflection of her own. *Leave it to government to make everything uniformly boring,* she thought to herself as she moved about the desks and cabinets. The good news was that, because the layout was the same, she could assume that filing cabinets were located in the same general vicinity as they were in the business licenses department. She was right. She pulled open the handle of the closest drawer. It did not move. Sarah bit her lip. *Oh, no, they're locked,* she said to herself. This was turning out to be an unsuccessful mission. She looked around. *Where are the keys?* She wondered. Her intuition told her that the department administrative assistant was probably responsible for locking up the cabinets at night. That meant Sarah only had to locate the desk of the assistant, and she'd probably be able to get her hands on the keys. That is if the assistant didn't keep them on the same key ring as his or her car keys. No, that was against policy, because if the assistant were sick no one would be able to get into the cabinets. She grew confident. Yes, the keys were definitely around here somewhere.

She determined that the workstation closest to the manager's office was probably the assistant's. She checked the desk drawers. They were locked. *Where would someone hide keys?* She racked her brain. They had to be around here somewhere. She looked under the overhead bin to see if the keys were hanging from a hook. No luck. She felt under the desk surface. No luck again. She sat on the assistant's chair, trying to get a feel for how the person organized the workspace. *Wow, this chair is comfortable,* thought Sarah. *I'll have to requisition one of these.* She made a mental note before continuing her task.

She checked her watch. 6:30 PM. She'd already been here fifteen minutes and achieved exactly nothing. *Think, think,* she told herself. The administrative assistant's workstation was well organized. There were containers for pens, elastics, bull clips and even a deep ceramic bowl of paperclips. *Aha!* thought Sarah, and plunged her hand deep into the bowl and pulling out the keys. *Yes!!* She briefly gave herself a mental pat on the back before jumping out of the chair to attack the cabinets. The drawers opened immediately, although somewhat noisily. She paused and looked around, listening for signs of other life. She resolved to proceed quietly and quickly. Every minute she spent here brought her one step closer to being discovered, and she was not prepared to face the repercussions.

She started alphabetically but quickly realized that she would not achieve her goals this way. Some of the files were decades old, and she was looking for recent evidence of wrong-doing, whatever that was. She had to be more methodical and strategic.

She took a closer look at the file folders. The older ones were manila colored, and had labels that had clearly been made with a typewriter using a courier font. Not only that, the labels' glue was getting old and many were peeling. In contrast, the newer folders were fresh and boldly colored in blue, purple, green and yellow and had plastic film labels made with a newer type of label maker. She resolved to focus only on the newer files. Still, she recognized that this would take some time, which she did not have. She flipped quickly through the building permit files. Some general contractors had hired Sturdy Roofing Installations, but others were listed as well: Able Roofing, Enzo's Roof and Shingle, Salwat's Building Contractors.

After another twenty minutes, she was able to put together a fistful of construction project files for which building permits had been issued within the last five years, and where Sturdy had been hired as the roofer. As she leafed through the documents in the files, she saw that each showed the signature of Charles Kingly attesting to the completion of the work, and the signature of the building inspector verifying that the workmanship had been performed in accordance with the local building code.

In all, she had retrieved fourteen files. In five cases, the building inspector was Steve Haddock, three were Jonas Frey, and in six cases it was Bill Trimly. Everything appeared to be in order. She checked the time on a wall clock. 7:15 PM. That was it; she had to leave. The cleaning crew would arrive shortly. She returned the files to their alphabetical places in the cabinet and locked it before burying the keys deep into the dish of paperclips. It was only once she'd returned to her own desk that she relaxed. She shut down her computer, and put away her work. She would call Marilee with an update tomorrow. Right now she needed a nice glass of red wine and a bubble bath to relieve her stress. She hadn't realized that detecting could be so nerve-racking!

Chapter 19

▼

Sarah and Marilee had a lot to update each other on, and agreed to meet for lunch at a local soup and sandwich shop that was ten minutes from Sarah's workplace. Marilee recognized that Sarah had a set lunch hour, and was always careful to respect that. Thankfully, the place was unpopular (although the shop's management probably weren't very happy about that), and they were able to find a table where they could talk quietly with little chance of being overheard. The last thing Sarah needed was for someone to find out that she'd been snooping in government files. That was a sure way to get fired in no time flat. But now that it was over, she was excited to be able to share her information with Marilee, such as it was.

They arrived at about the same time, placed their orders and took them back to the secluded table.

"You first," said Marilee. She couldn't wait to hear about Sarah's adventures.

"Okay," said Sarah, and launched into a detailed description of her movements, including how fast her heart was beating as she sleuthed in the building permit office.

Marilee was suitably impressed, and told her so. The picture that Sarah conjured in Marilee's mind was so vivid; she felt she had been there herself.

"So what did you find out?" Marilee was dying to know.

Sarah pouted. "Unfortunately, very little. I found a lot of records, but nothing suspicious."

"Okay. Tell me what you did see. What did the records show?"

"Once I narrowed it down to building construction where Sturdy was the roofer, I found fourteen files for recently finished projects. Charles Kingly signed for the completion of the work, and three different inspectors signed off on the various projects. That ties with my understanding of the building permit department. They have three staff inspectors. They are each assigned certain construction sites to inspect. Whoever is assigned a building site completes the inspection and signs the inspection report. I'm sorry, Marilee, but it all seems above board to me." She shrugged. "I don't know what else I could have checked."

"Hmm." Marilee thought for a moment. "So be it. I truly thought we would find some proof of illegal activity." She mulled the thought over in her mind, and decided to put it aside for the moment. She said appreciatively, "You did a great job, Sarah, and I hope I never ask you to do something like that again. It's not right of me to ask you to risk your job to help with my amateur detective work." She said seriously. She smiled, "But I'm glad you did it, anyway." They both laughed. Now that it was over, it was easy to view it as a simple transgression, like a dare or prank, but they both knew the truth. It had been a crazy thing to do to achieve their objective. Sarah could have lost her job over it. But, they had needed to know whether Sturdy Roofing Installations were doing something illegal and now they knew.

Chapter 20

▼

Unbeknownst to Marilee, Friday would turn out to be a busy day for her. It was the beginning of the Mother's Day weekend, and, as far as she knew, her day would consist of going to work in the morning and picking up her mother from the airport in the late afternoon.

Around nine o'clock, George called with news about the memory card. What he told her was disappointing. To her relief, the only fingerprints on the card had been Stanford's and hers, as they had expected, but that was not the disappointing part. It appeared that the card contained 154 pictures covering the period from the fall of the previous year to this spring. The subjects of the shots were as expected, various gardens with heady displays of glorious color and contrasting plantings. Unfortunately, the forensic analysts were not enthralled by the beauty of the shots and would have preferred images that provided some clue as to their owner's killer.

Marilee was stumped. She was, of course, grateful that George had shared this information with her, but didn't see what could be done with it. On a long shot, she offered again to view the pictures with the police to see if she could help in any way.

George chuckled. "I think we can handle it, Marilee."

"Are there any pictures where the images are blurry or unclear? I could help you determine what plants they are. Okay, not that I know how that would help, I agree." She offered again.

On the other end of the phone line, she could sense George considering her offer. "Okay," he said. "It can't hurt. I'll call you my botanical expert." He laughed out loud. "I guess it can't be any worse than calling in a fortuneteller or mystic, like some police forces have done." He gave another snort of laughter, oblivious to how Marilee would receive the comment. Here she was, offering up her valuable time, and he was comparing her, unfairly, to mystics and card-readers. She remained silent. Frankly, she was glad to be able to help, and she was fairly certain that there would be time to straighten George out on the fortuneteller comparison later. She made a mental note to address it at a later time. After all, botany was a scientific discipline.

They agreed that she would come down to the station after lunch the same afternoon, so just after one o'clock Marilee jumped into her FJ Cruiser and raced to headquarters. No one could say she wasn't doing her bit to help stop crime, but her speed could easily have resulted in one or two tickets as she made her way to Hampton Avenue. George had directed her to ask for Jim Peterson when she arrived, and she did so as she checked in with the desk sergeant.

Jim appeared shortly, wearing his standard dark gray suit, white shirt and tie. Just to complete the picture, Marilee checked his shoes to see if they were properly polished. They were. She grinned as she shook his proffered hand and followed him into the bowels of the building 'where the real police work is done'.

In truth, as they entered the elevator, they did not head down, but rather up to the third floor, where Jim again took the lead and showed Marilee into a crowded boardroom filled with computers and staff. As she entered, she took in the entire scene: white boards on the walls outlining clues and other salient points, newspaper cuttings, photos of Stanford Platson, his wife Glenda, Dierdre and Tom Dearling. She noted that the photo of Glenda was an older one that predated the murder and did not reflect her new look. The table was weighted with stacks of paper, and waste paper baskets overflowed with shredded documents. Abutting one wall was a gray credenza carrying the remains of what appeared to three days' worth of lunches. Marilee hoped this was not the case, or the police department would soon be overrun with mice. A tray of cookies sat untouched in the center of the table.

Jim dispensed with introductions, Marilee presumed, because he felt her visit would be short-lived or that it would serve no purpose (she decided not to take offense) and offered her a seat next to a forensic analyst, whom he introduced as Rebecca.

As he sat, he asked Marilee where the card had eventually been found. She explained the visit from Glenda Platson, followed by her own frustration that this important clue had not been located, her determination to look for it, the search process she used to find it, and where she found it. When George came to pick it up, he had assigned two officers to comb the area again to check for other evidence in the same location. They had remained tight-lipped when asked by employees regarding the purpose of their search. No mention of the secured memory card was made, and employees were left to assume the card remained missing. No additional evidence was found.

Jim nodded throughout her description of the chain of events. "Still," he said, "I wonder how it ended up in the chokeberry bush. Shouldn't the card have remained in the camera? Why remove it?"

Marilee shrugged. She would leave it to Jim and George to come up with theories to explain it. All she knew was that she was here and ready to look at photos. She glanced at Jim and Rebecca expectantly her posture erect and her hands folded peacefully in her lap. Rebecca, in the meantime, had remained quiet, behavior that, in all probability, had been instilled in her during intensive disciplinary training dictating that one should remain silent until spoke to. Marilee inferred that she was of lower rank than Jim, and was waiting to be addressed.

Jim resolved to put his question to George at a later time, making a notation in his pad to remind him. As he looked up again, both women were looking at him expectantly.

"Okay, let's get started. Marilee, I want to remind you that the card contains 154 pictures, and we may want to cycle through them a few times, so I hope you will be able to spend a bit of time here. What we are planning to do is to go through the pictures fairly quickly the first time. As Rebecca and I have already reviewed them thoroughly, we will watch as you review them for the first time. You know that these are all pictures of either flowers or gardens, so we do not expect commentary on each photo, unless you find a trend or some other odd theme that carries through them. Are you ready to get started?"

Marilee nodded. This was so exhilarating! Not normally one to become easily excited, but helping the police to catch a killer was one event in her life she would always remember.

"Okay, Rebecca. Please start from the beginning. Marilee, you will notice that these go back to last fall."

Marilee paid close attention to each photo as Rebecca scrolled methodically through them, giving her one or two seconds to view each one before moving on to the next screen. Not having previously seen any of Stanford's pictures, she was impressed with the clarity and detail he had captured, especially in macro shots of individual flowers. Images of vibrant pink, lemon and mango colored roses appeared and disappeared just as quickly, replaced by rust-colored chrysanthemums, pink Japanese anemones and lavender asters. Other images captured the gentle devolution of late summer into fall. He had done an excellent job of capturing the colorful transition of maple trees as their leaves turned to gold through rust then shades of pink, and burning bushes with their slender brilliant-red fall leaves.

After about five minutes they had completely scrolled through the images. Sadness overcame Marilee as she realized that the person who had captured these lovely images was no longer among the living. He may not have been a very noticeable or accomplished man, but he had created these pictures, and for that he was a loss to this world. Jim interrupted her reverie.

"So, Marilee, did you see anything that seemed odd, something that might help our investigation?" He assumed not, since Marilee had remained silent the first time through. He drummed his thick fingers on the wooden table.

"Nothing that was evident." She realized then how difficult it must be for police officers that dealt with these types of frustrating clues every day. How could they even tell what evidence was valuable and what was not? She had seen television shows where cigarette butts and candy wrappers were collected from the scene, and the police had to determine which of them, if any, had any significance. Thank goodness Sandalwood had few murders.

"Is it possible that we could narrow it down to the last fifty or so? I mean, if he snapped a picture of someone doing something illegal, for example, and they saw him take the picture, they would have acted fairly quickly to cover their tracks, right? In which case, I think we should ignore photos Stanford took more than, for example, two or three months ago." Marilee paused, looking at Jim and Rebecca to see if they agreed with her suggestion and logic. Jim and Melissa looked at each other searchingly.

"So are you saying that you feel that we should dispense with looking at the pictures from the fall and winter, and focus on the more recent ones?" clarified Melissa.

"Yes. Is there any way to tell when the photos were taken? Like some sort of date stamp?" She did not want to show her ignorance, but Marilee did not own a digital camera, and had no idea how much and what type of information was contained on a memory card.

"Actually, yes. Using the right software, we can access all of the data that accompanies each picture. That includes the date, as well as information that is of more interest to a photographer, such as whether the focus was automatic or manual, the shutter speed, the aperture setting, graphics quality and a number of other features."

"Great. So let's look at the ones after January 1, to pick a date." They waited until Melissa accessed the right software and had scrolled through the pictures and accompanying data to find the first picture taken after the arbitrarily selected date.

"According to this information, the first pictures he took this year are dated mid-March. See here," she pointed at the screen, "the first picture is of some purple crocuses in the snow." She pointed out that the previous photo was dated late November.

"Marilee," added Jim, "if we proceed with your hypothesis, we should look only at the photos from mid-March onward. Rebecca, how many does that include?"

"Twenty seven."

They scrolled through the pertinent images, this time studying each one meticulously. Only when they all agreed that they did not see anything suspicious did they move on to the next one. When they neared the middle of the bunch Marilee's attention was drawn from the evident subject, tulips and such, to the background. In fact, as they continued, she counted nine pictures contained tulips in the foreground against a background of star magnolia, behind which variations in gray tones gave a vague outline of two figures. Marilee explained her impression to Jim and Rebecca, and together they pored over the nine images for a third and fourth time. They agreed that it did indeed appear that the selected shots captured blurry images of two or three people in the background.

It soon became apparent that the others in the room had become aware of the new development, and a flurry of questions erupted to which no one seemed to have the answers. At some point, George must have been called, because he appeared in the doorway to be updated and participate in the discussion.

"Where was that shot taken?" "Does anyone recognize those people?" "Was that taken in a park? Does anyone know what park?" Questions flew through the air with no apparent answers.

"Does the camera record where he took the photo?" Marilee asked Rebecca hopefully.

"Some cameras permit the photographer to key in subject details, such as the names of people or a location. Mr. Platson's camera had that feature, but he did not use it." she pointed at the screen where the information would have been displayed. *So that wasn't a stupid question,* thought Marilee, relieved, but feeling definitely out of touch with today's technological advances. *Maybe I should buy a digital camera,* she thought, and immediately discarded the idea. *I'll get one when I'm good and ready,* she decided, resolving not to take on the consumer mentality that permitted manufacturers to make and market a new model every year to a public that craved 'the latest' this or that.

Apparently Rebecca had arisen and moved to join an earnest conversation in one corner of the room with George and Jim while Marilee ruminated about upgrading to the new millennium. Now, from what Marilee could make out, they were discussing the possibility of enhancing the images to obtain greater definition of the people in the background of the shots.

"How long will that take?" George asked pressingly.

"Depends. It may take a couple of weeks or more. And we may have to request help from the regional forensic unit. I'm sorry, but we don't have the right expertise here, George." Rebecca was more circumspect and knew the limitations of their local resources. They were, after all, a small community police force and did not have the luxury of employing officers with narrow specializations.

Knowing her to be right, George looked annoyed. "Damn it, get them on this right away. I don't want to have to say that a murderer continues to be loose because we don't have the tools to work the clues. Is that clear? And Rebecca, get an estimated time for them to complete this analysis, will you?" She nodded respectfully and marched efficiently out of the room, presumably to place a call before transmitting the pertinent images to the regional unit over a secure connection.

It wasn't until this moment that George and Jim noticed that Marilee was still sitting in the conference room. They had entirely forgotten about her. She had remained silent while the whole brouhaha surrounded her and subsided. George approached her.

"Thanks for coming down to the station, Marilee. You have been immensely helpful. I can't tell you how valuable your input has been. I don't know how we missed it, but I guess, as my botanical expert," he chuckled at that, "you noticed that the shot was not set against a background of trees but rather of people." He strolled with her to the elevator and took her back to the lobby.

"I'll have to buy you lunch sometime," he offered graciously. She smiled. "I'm pleased to have been of some help. I look forward to lunch." she replied easily before returning to her car. She checked the clock on the dashboard. Yikes, she hadn't realized that the afternoon had flown so quickly. She smiled to herself. But it had sure been invigorating! She threw the shift knob into reverse, backed out of the space and headed to the airport. She didn't want to keep her poor mom waiting. They had planned this visit for some time and it would not do to show up late.

~

Deep in thought, George headed back to the conference room and met Jim in the narrow corridor, so George altered his plan and invited him back to his office, where they both took a seat. Finally, they had a development they could sink their teeth into that might surface one or two useful leads. Jim remembered his earlier question about how the camera's memory card could possibly have been found so far from the original search area. He described the area again to George, who, of course, also had it fresh in his mind from his recent visit to the garden center.

"I find it so odd that the card was not actually in the camera. How could that have happened?"

"Hmm, I see what you mean."

"In my opinion, the card should have been kept in the camera. What benefit was it to have a camera without a memory card and to carry a loose memory card, presumably, in his pocket?"

"Okay, in case it's of any value to the investigation, which remains to be seen," George raised a skeptical eyebrow at Jim, "let's review for a moment what reasons Platson might have had to remove the card from the camera, or, not to be presumptuous, to carry the card separate from the camera."

Jim considered. To his way of thinking, there was no good reason for it, as he had already mentioned to George. As a result, he waited for George to venture the first reason.

George rubbed his stubbly chin thoughtfully. "My personal observation ties with yours, Jim. I would not want to carry a memory card separate from my camera unless I had a storage case to place it in to protect it from damage. As you know, the copper contact strips are delicate and easy to mar, making them susceptible to damage, which would render the card useless. To a person like Platson, in fact, to anyone, I imagine, if one already has images on the card, this would be aggravating, as the images may become irretrievable and potentially lost. Presumably Platson knew this." He walked around his desk and ran his fingers through his hair. "All right, putting that aside, reasons to remove the card, or keep it separate: it's full, it's damaged, he wants to give it to someone, he wants to remind himself to do something with it, he dropped it and didn't want to replace it into the camera without cleaning it to avoid damaging the camera. Stop me when I get to a reason you find palatable, will you Jim?" He waited silently, giving Jim a chance to digest the suggestions before responding.

"You haven't mentioned one yet, although that last one has some merit. So what are you saying?"

George sighed. "I think that we can't always understand why people do what they do, Jim. While it may not make sense to us, I believe that Platson had removed the card from the camera with the intention of doing something with it, and most probably placed it in his overcoat pocket. When he was murdered, the loose card flew from his pocket and landed in the garden center bushes. If there is any significance to the card having been in Platson's pocket, we haven't found it. I suggest we focus our investigation on the contents of the card for now. Like I said, we can't always understand why people do what they do. Do you agree?"

Jim nodded, resigned. It was true, sometimes in an investigation one read significance into things that had none. He decided that George was right. First things first: focus on the images on the card. He did, however, resolve to keep the issue of why the card had been loose in the back of his mind, to dwell on when he was otherwise idle. Which was never. He chuckled and rose from his chair to head back to the conference room and check in with Rebecca.

"Changing subjects, while we wait for forensics to digitally enhance the photos, Jim, what are you planning for your next steps?"

Jim stood near the door, his hand resting on the brushed aluminum knob. "I was thinking I'd pay a surprise visit to the widow Platson to show her the photos and ask her if she recognizes the area in which they were taken. If not, she might be able to shed some light on which parks and areas Platson made a habit of frequenting, or failing that, if he kept a record or had mentioned to her where he was going that day."

"Great idea, Jim. Let me know what you find out." He paused and reconsidered. "Before you do that, I have an idea I want to pass by you."

He asked Jim to close the door before continuing.

~

The Mother's Day weekend brought beautiful blue skies, warm days and Marilee's mother. Travelers, both mothers and families, crowded the airport, journeying to connect for the special day. Because Marilee's mother lived in Florida, and Marilee visited her often during the winter months, they had seen each other less than two months ago. Still, with the change of seasons, it seemed like a year had passed (at least to Marilee), and, after spotting each other in the dense throng, they greeted each other enthusiastically.

Stephanie was excited to visit her daughter. A popular widow with a busy social calendar and innumerable friends, she rarely traveled to see Marilee in Sandalwood, so this visit was a delight for them both.

Relieving her mother of her heavy bags, Marilee directed her to the parked car. Along the way they chatted animatedly about recent events in their lives and brought each other up to date. As usual, Stephanie asked whether Marilee was seeing anyone. Thankfully, Marilee never let the question goad her, and answered simply that, no, there was no one in her life at the moment. Her mother sighed in exasperation. Likely there was some unspoken wish to see her only child happily married and with children of her own. Considering Marilee was in her forties, it was unlikely that there were offspring in her future, but her mother held out hope. Once, in her twenties, they had come close, and her mother's reminiscences of what might have been undoubtedly frequently reminded her to inquire into Marilee's status.

The (ancient, Marilee would say) history of it was this: at the age of twenty-four, Marilee had met and married a charming, quick-witted, sandy-haired dentist with green eyes the color of a lush spring meadow, and they had both felt their union would be for forever. That is, until Marilee found that some of his weekend 'emergency' appointments were anything but, and had sent him packing. Including the time they had dated, the entire relationship had lasted a mere three years. It had been heartbreaking for Marilee, not to mention her mother, who had observed in silence. Marilee resolved never to be taken in again, and if she ever ventured down that path for a second time, it would be after a long engagement and thorough check of both her feelings and his commitment. One divorce could be put down to a mistake, but two? She felt it would be inexcusable, and wanted to avoid it at all cost. Of course, that scenario was two leaps from where she currently was, since a second marriage was not even in the offing. Still, just the idea of it made her exceedingly cautious.

Stephanie was a well-preserved woman in her mid-sixties. Her twinkling blue eyes had the effect of making her the center of attention at many gatherings, and her friendly personality completed the picture. A shock of silvery-white hair was styled simply by brushing it back from her forehead. It had a natural wave and stayed just as she had brushed it. The elegant look suited her. Lucky her, Marilee had always thought, as she had looked at her thin strands in the mirror. Her own hair could have used more volume to give it some sort of life without her primping and fussing over it every day. She had since dispensed with making comparisons. What was the point? You had what God gave you, that was all. No point whining about it.

Her father had died at the age of sixty-two as the result of an aneurysm on a lengthy business flight from Miami to San Diego. It had been a rough time for Stephanie and Marilee, but time had helped them get over the pain. It was now six years ago, and wife and daughter had recovered and moved on with their lives, although it had no doubt been harder on Stephanie, who now had to adjust to living alone in Florida. Thankfully, her friends had quickly rallied around her and helped her overcome the loneliness with their attention and invitations.

Upon arrival at home, Marilee installed her mother's suitcases in the second bedroom and made her way into the kitchen to make coffee. Her mother, used to the routine, had already made herself comfortable in the breakfast nook, where she munched lemon biscuits retrieved from the cupboard, being careful to avoid spilling crumbs on the floor. Always interested in what was going on, Cinder padded in silently and jumped on Stephanie's lap to make himself comfortable. She enjoyed the easy affection of the charcoal colored cat. His ears flattened and his eyes pulled back as she petted his head heavily. He usually preferred a lighter touch, but was willing to take what he could get. When no treats appeared to be coming his way, he eventually pounced onto the floor and made his way into the living room to find a sunbeam where he could curl up on the warm floor.

"So how's the plant business?" she was always on the lookout for danger signs in Marilee's professional and personal life, and Marilee knew she was in for the third degree as her mother went through her mental 'Marilee' status checklist. It was like a pre-flight cockpit check, thought Marilee with a chuckle. *Oil pressure? Check! Flaps? Check! Fuel level? Check!* Her mother was making sure the 'engine' of Marilee's life was in full functioning order. It was funny, but Marilee also knew it came from love and concern for her well being, so she endured the periodic checkup.

"It's fine, Mom. Really," she said as she watched her mother's eyebrows raise, looking for reassurance. "If you want, I'll take you to Green Horizons tomorrow and I'll show you the new arrivals. Quite a few plants are in bloom now, so it will be great to see." Thankfully, her mother was an interested gardener, and enjoyed plant talk, although Marilee knew that her question had been financial, not plant oriented.

"That would be great." Marilee made the offer every visit, and Stephanie took her up on it every time. She loved the atmosphere of the masses of burgeoning greenery, and looked forward to seeing the long-term staffers again, some of whom she had become quite fond.

But there was some news her mother did not know, Marilee suspected. It was highly unlikely that she had heard about the death at Green Horizons. If she had, it would have been only in the vaguest terms. Not that the murder of a fellow human being should be treated lightly, but it was interesting news. Marilee silently asked Stanford Platson for forgiveness before launching into the story for her mother's benefit.

An observer would have noted that the expression on Stephanie's face transform from disbelief, to shock, to indignation, to fear as she heard the details of poor Stanford's demise. She did not know him, but that made little difference to her reaction. She was aghast at the knowledge that such a thing had, one, happened, two, happened in such close proximity to her daughter, and, three, that the killer had not yet been apprehended. *Gees, wait until I tell her that I've been assisting in the investigation, she'll really go green around the gills.* She thought she'd let the basic story sink in before she would describe the details of her own activities.

However, now that Stephanie's important questions were out of the way, and despite being aghast over Marilee's local crime story, Stephanie was beginning to show the signs of having spent the last several hours traveling. Marilee realized she'd have to save the rest of her tales for the morning, which was fine. The visit was planned for several days, and there would be plenty of time for a more detailed discussion later. Her mother would, no doubt, also have many questions, questions she was too tired to express this evening.

Chapter 21

▼

In the morning her mother was a new person. Marilee noted with concern how much the travel must be wearing on her, and wondered how much longer she could enjoy her mother's periodic visits. If she had voiced those concerns, she knew her mother would have told her she was speaking nonsense; that she was fit as a fiddle and fully able to travel. And, of course, in the short term this was true. She was still very healthy, no doubt due to her active calendar, and was sharp as a tack. But it did not keep Marilee from noticing the inevitable: that it would be she who would visit her mother in Florida more and more, and her mother's visits to Sandalwood would eventually peter out as the travel increasingly wore on her. Taking that thought one step further, she acknowledged that she loved her mother dearly, and dreaded the thought that one day, she would no longer have the pleasure of her company.

As her mother entered the kitchen, Marilee banned the negative thoughts from her mind, flipped the eggs in the pan and popped two slices of whole-wheat bread into the toaster. The eggs were almost ready and she looked forward to eating a cozy breakfast with her mother.

"Good morning, Mom. Did you sleep well?"

"Good morning, Marilee. Yes, thanks, I did. I slept the sleep of the dead, as they say. You know, it's not the flight itself that does it, but all the rushing and waiting and standing around in airports that drains me. I was totally beat yesterday. Sorry about that, sweetie. But a restful night's sleep has done me good." she said as she pulled the orange juice container from the refrigerator to pour them both a glass.

The toast popped and Marilee dropped the hot slices nimbly on two plates. She placed two more in the slots before placing the plates on the table alongside a jar of black currant jam, which they both liked immensely, almost to the exclusion of all other jams.

Stephanie walked around the table to sit near the window, pulling the local Sandalwood Chronicle towards her to read the headlines. After having spent a number of visits with Marilee in the past, she liked to think she knew a fair number of the local citizenry, and she was checking to see if any of them appeared in today's issue of the community newspaper. As she glanced over the headlines, her eyes rested on a small story near the bottom of the page. 'Murder of local accountant remains unsolved' ran the headline. Her face was shocked as she read the horrifying details of the crime, despite Marilee's recounting of the events the previous evening. Marilee walked toward the table and placed the 'over easy' eggs on their plates being careful not to burn herself or her mother with the frying pan.

She had already seen the headline, and noticed that her mother was absorbing the details she herself had failed to cover in last night's brief summary of the crime. After a moment's consideration, she determined that now was as good a time as any to drop the other shoe. "Mom," she started warily, "I've been doing some investigating on that case, too."

Marilee glanced at her to gauge her mother's reaction. Stephanie was regarding her with a steady eye. "What are you playing at, Marilee?" she asked. "Haven't the police told you that murder is a dangerous game?" She was not angry, but Marilee could tell she was cautiously assessing Marilee's involvement. She sighed and sat down on the nearest chair, placing the hot frying pan on a dishtowel before launching into the details she had not had time to express yesterday. It would have been too much to unload onto an unsuspecting, weary traveler.

"Yes, the detective on the case has warned me to stay away from it." She might as well admit up front that she knew that what she was doing was unwise.

Her mother paused to read the expression on Marilee's face, and laughed in resignation; there was no helping it. Whatever her daughter set her mind to, she would do. She just hoped she would stay safe while doing it. "I could always tell when you were dying to tell me something. So spill it. What have you been up to? I can't very well chastise you over something you've clearly already done, and from what I can see, you're still in one piece."

Marilee was relieved. It would have been so much harder to explain her activities if her mother had decided to be stern and unaccepting.

So, over breakfast, Marilee spilled out the entire story, not yesterday's abbreviated version. She included how she had linked the murder to a break-in at the victim's widow's house, raised the alarm about Tom Dearling, convinced her friend Sarah to commit a misdemeanor by searching building permit files for incriminating information, found the missing memory card, and helped the police identify potentially valuable information on the card.

When she was finished she realized she had forgotten to breathe while reciting the detailed chain of events to her mother. As she inhaled to restore normal breathing, her mother had a chance to digest it all.

"Wow, Marilee, that's pretty impressive, even if I do say that you're taking some risks, since this criminal is still at large. And it sounds like you've made some great contributions to the police's investigation." She paused to study her daughter. "Hmm. Maybe you chose the wrong second career," she ventured. "Maybe you should have pursued a career in law enforcement, rather than landscaping and gardening," she said mischievously. "It seems to me that you're doing a fine job of helping solve this case."

Marilee wiped the butter and jam from her fingers and placed her head in her hands. "Yes, but the case is again at a standstill. If the police can't enhance the images on the photos, we will be back to square one." She looked at her mother. "I might have found police work too frustrating, I think, Mom. I find it irritating to have so little in the way of information and clues to work with. Although, if I were a police officer, I would have greater flexibility to question and interview suspects, and could gather more information that way." She sighed, resigned to solve this crime from the sidelines. "Not only that, but who wants to get up in the middle of the night to investigate some late night shooting? Not me!!"

Her mother nodded in acknowledgment, a smile playing on her lips. She knew Marilee valued her sleep.

"So what clues do you have to work with?" Her mother was clearly getting into the mood, albeit without having acknowledged it. Marilee watched as she helped herself to a second piece of toast and halved it, using one half to sop up the runny egg yolk and spreading butter and jam on the other half.

Marilee listed points on her fingers: "First, the police may or may not have been able to lift fingerprints from the cultivator's claws. They haven't told me, not that I expected them to, but it would be good to know if that evidence exists. Second, the intruder at Glenda Platson's home left DNA behind when he ransacked her home. However, this piece of information is useless until it can be compared to DNA extracted from a likely suspect. Third, I have not yet heard from Glenda whether she has located any clues on Stan's PC. Fourth, we have a memory card with blurry photos on it." She paused to check whether she had missed anything. She felt she had summed it up pretty well.

"I think that's about it. I mean, we still have a suspect that has refused to give a DNA sample for whatever reason. Oh yes, and I believe that there are three possible suspects. One is the illegitimate son that I just mentioned, the one that refused to provide a mouth swab for DNA comparison. The second is the victim's wife, who stands to benefit in a number of ways from his death. The third, which I have not been able to substantiate in any way beyond my own suspicions, is Sturdy Roofing Installations, most notably Charles Kingly, or a business client. I guess I should add a fourth, although I'm not sold on this one. Jaz is also a suspect in the police's eyes, because she found the body. They believe that she might have been the person to fatally wound him with the garden tool. I have to admit it is possible, because, like most of the people at the garden center, she has developed some impressive upper body strength through her work and would have been able to wield the weapon in such a way as to kill him with one stroke. Personally, I don't think she would hurt a fly, but I guess you never know."

Stephanie slid her reading glasses down her nose to see her daughter more clearly and rested her head on her palm as a wisp of white hair fell from behind one ear.

"This is fascinating. I would remind you again to leave it to the police, but I can see that you're deeply engrossed in finding out who committed the murder." She paused to consider.

"Since you are intent on ignoring my advice anyway, here are my thoughts." Knowing her mother to have sharp insights, Marilee waited to hear her contribution.

"First, the DNA and fingerprints are the domain of the police, and you will have a hard time if you think you are in a position to use this information to track down the criminal. Second, you should follow up with Glenda to find out if she found any further incriminating information on her husband's PC. That's easy enough to do, although I recommend that you do this in person, not over the phone. As she is still a suspect, you will want to see her expression when she gives you her answers, to determine her level of honesty and credibility."

"Third, the card and the blurry photos." She reread the article. "What has the public been told about this card?"

"I was asked by the detective not to say a word to anyone about finding it, and so I haven't. Only to you, today."

"I wonder why the perpetrator didn't come looking for it in your garden center when he heard it had not been found? It is a logical step after searching Platson's house." She looked questioningly at Marilee over the stylish charcoal rims of her glasses.

"Good observation. Maybe he did. It's possible that he went to the garden center one night and looked for it and did not find it. I don't have any security cameras or motion detectors or Rottweilers guarding it, as you know. The only protection is a locked gate so that enterprising people can't back their cars in and fill up a trailer with plant stock or a load of soil at night. That said, anyone could park his car at the side of the road in the middle of the night and walk in to take a look for the card. And the killer would know exactly where to look."

Now that the thought had been created, it troubled Marilee. Perhaps some intruder *had* prowled through the garden center at night, perhaps several nights, to find the errant card. What a creepy thought. Ugh. A shiver ran up her spine. She shook herself.

Stephanie meanwhile continued to look thoughtful. "Have the police considered setting a trap?"

"What do you mean, Mom?"

"Let's assume for a moment that Platson was killed because he had captured some illegal or private activity on his digital camera. How would the criminal know that the pictures had turned out blurry? Presumably, the killer believes that the pictures show clear images of whatever he was doing in the park. Otherwise, he would not have killed Platson. So he eliminated a witness linking him to the crime, but when he opened the camera, he was shocked to find that the photographic evidence was missing. Keep in mind that he had very little time, as he had committed the crime during broad daylight, and during business hours too, so presumably there were other people nearby. He may have looked around for a few minutes before deciding he had run out of time. Later, when he had given it some thought, he decided to burglarize Platson's house in the hopes of finding the card there. And that is probably why the houseplants were all overturned and everything had been thoroughly searched. He was assuming Platson had recognized what was going on in the pictures, and that he had hidden the card in case something happened."

She paused to let it sink in. She looked at Marilee inquisitively. "What do you think? Based on everything you know, is it possible that might have happened?"

Marilee mulled it over. Certainly, it would explain everything so far. "Yes, that would tie. So what are you suggesting?" She remembered that her mother had started this conversation by suggesting some sort of trap be set up to catch the killer.

"So, don't you see? The killer thinks the photos are clear. He does not know that they are blurry and that only the plants in the foreground are clear. Even if the police don't manage to enhance them, the trump card is in your and the police's hands. You can bluff him into exposing himself!" she finished, elated with her elaborate scheme.

Her daughter was just as elated. It was an excellent idea, and reminded her of the brief discussion she had had with Trent in the days following the murder. There was only one problem now: how to set a trap. She would have to discuss this idea with George and obtain his collaboration. She leaned over and wrapped an arm around her mother. "I knew there was a reason I invited you here," she said jokingly planting a big kiss on her cheek. Her mother laughed. She was delighted to play a small part in solving this little murder mystery.

Once they'd recovered from the giddiness of their discovery, she looked earnestly into her daughter's eyes, "But, Marilee, I have to tell you, please be careful. The police weren't joking when they warned you to stay out of it. I know it will do no good for me to tell you the same thing, because I know you, but please don't put yourself at unnecessary risk. I love you and I wouldn't like to have to visit you in the morgue." She grinned at the macabre image she had painted. She hoped Marilee got her point.

~

After taking her mother to Green Horizons in the morning and spending a few hours, her mother chatting with the staff, she checking her orders and checking in with Pete and Jane, she took her mother home for a much needed rest while she drove off to visit Glenda Platson. Hopefully, Glenda would be at home, and Marilee would be able to have a brief conversation with her about Stan's PC, and to check whether she had received any more unwelcome visitors.

A tall man who appeared to be in his mid fifties opened the door. Marilee was startled for a moment. It took a few seconds for her to register that the person standing before her was Jack Talbot, Glenda's new love interest.

She held out her hand in greeting, "Hello, I'm Marilee Bright," she explained.

"Hi there, I'm Jack Talbot." A huge smile spread across his face. "I assume you're here to see Glenda." He turned to see if she'd heard the doorbell and was heading towards them. She hadn't.

"Come in, please. I'll get her for you." As Marilee stepped inside, he excused himself and headed upstairs to find Glenda.

My, my, he's certainly made himself comfortable, she commented to herself, noticing the blue, fleece slippers as he stepped lightly up the carpeted stairs. *I'll bet his toothbrush is sitting in a cup by the bathroom sink, too.*

A moment later, Glenda descended the stairs, rather embarrassed. It appeared she had not expected anyone to come calling. Perhaps her embarrassment was due to being found out for having a new man in her life and in her home, although, based on the rumors floating around Sandalwood, the first did not appear to be a secret. Marilee decided not to comment, preferring rather, if anything were going to be said, that Glenda would be the one to broach the topic.

Glenda invited her in for a cup of coffee. Marilee accepted and followed her to the kitchen. Glenda removed the remains of a cozy lunch of potato salad and pork chops to the counter to make room for them to sit without being surrounded by the sights and smells of the leftover food. For the first time, Marilee's stomach growled and she notice that she hadn't eaten since breakfast. She hoped her mother would take the initiative and make herself something at Marilee's home. The thought passed. Her mother was no shy visitor and could take care of herself quite well. Glenda set the kettle on and went about gathering the items they would need for coffee.

Seated, watching her, Marilee said, "I came to ask about Stanford's computer. The last time we spoke, you were concerned about having another burglary, and I suggested that you take a look through his computer and memory cards to see if you can find anything suspicious."

Glenda half turned and nodded in remembrance before returning to her task.

"Have you found anything?" A hot, black coffee was placed in front of her, along with milk in a small porcelain pitcher and a matching sugar bowl.

Glenda shook her head, unconcerned. "I haven't looked. You know, Abby came over and stayed with me for a few days, and that really relieved my worries about another break-in. She helped me set up bottles and wind chimes by all the doors so that we would be able to tell when someone breaks in. After that, I wasn't afraid anymore." She paused. "She only stayed a few days. Afterwards, I asked Jack to stay with me," she glanced surreptitiously at Marilee through downcast eyes to register her reaction. Marilee remained impassive. "and he's been a great comfort."

I'll bet he has, thought Marilee, but she kept her mouth shut. She didn't know why she felt uncharitable and prudish. *I should get out more,* she decided.

She thanked Glenda for the coffee and left.

In the car, she thought about these recent developments. Perhaps she should drop by to see George to fill him in on her findings and to discuss her mother's idea with him. Between the two of them, they should be able to come up with a plan.

Chapter 22

▼

The following morning Marilee left her mother to her own devices. She had made several friends on previous visits, and could prevail upon them for a ride, or get together for a visit. In fact, it would not be the first time that Marilee arrived home to a handful of her mother's friends playing bridge or backgammon.

Comforted by the thought that her mother would be able to occupy her time with her friends' company, and having warned her to keep quiet about the card, she headed to the police station to see George. This time she had called ahead to let him know she was coming, and to gauge his mood. By his welcoming tone, she determined that he would be agreeable when she arrived. She had told him she would be there in twenty minutes.

As usual, she checked in with the desk sergeant, who advised George that she had arrived, and to collect her from the lobby. It seemed such a laborious process. She could just as well show herself to his office, but she assumed such protocol prevented unwelcome and unexpected visitors from barging into the station with unknown intentions. *What is the world coming to that the police have to take such precautions,* she wondered.

George arrived all smiles. *He must be having a good day,* thought Marilee. *So much the better for me.* They headed towards his office for a private discussion.

"Thanks for seeing me, George. I appreciate your time and that you must have thousands of other things to do rather than talk to me," said Marilee.

"No problem, Marilee. Without you, we would have no new leads. Everything else had pretty much run dry when you came up with the memory card. We can't thank you enough for finding it."

"Thanks, George."

He offered her a cup of coffee. Like so many people with their own offices, he had his own coffee maker. The only drawback was that, unless he had a refrigerator, too, people had to make do with artificial whitener, not a favorite of Marilee's. Regardless, she accepted, adding 'cream' and sugar to the foam cup before stirring and taking a sip. She cringed but continued.

"I told you about Glenda's recent visit to me, when she mentioned that she was concerned about noises she heard at night at home. I decided enough is enough, and searched the garden center grounds thoroughly to find the memory card, as it seemed to be the key to the whole situation." She searched his face to see if the memory registered. He nodded.

"Go on."

"Before I found the card, I had suggested that she look through Stan's PC and other memory cards to see if there were any clues that would be helpful in identifying his murderer."

"Yes, we did too."

"I visited her yesterday to follow up on our conversation, and her reaction was very odd. Because she now has Jack Talbot living with her," he arched an eyebrow, "she feels safe and no longer cares about looking for helpful clues in Stan's computer files. Don't you think that's odd behavior for a grieving widow? You would think she would be overcome with concern to find the murderer, considering her *husband* was murdered."

"Yes, it is definitely odd. And, in fact, because we were unable to get her assistance with the computer files, we have officially requested the PC and files from her, to look through ourselves. I doubt we'll have to go as far as obtaining a court order to force her to provide us with the records. We will be visiting her in the morning to retrieve the records."

"That's a relief."

"Interesting tidbit about Jack Talbot, too. Has that been going on long?"

"From what I hear, she met him through her bridge club. Whether that was before or after Stanford died, I don't know."

"Interesting. We should be able to get more insight into that situation when we visit her house tomorrow." George made a note.

Marilee paused as she waited for him to finish. "Has the forensic group been able to digitally enhance the photos?"

"They're still working on it. It is a complex process that requires them to look at each pixel and determine what color it really is. They change the color of the pixel to the corresponding one adjacent to it. They have to do this with millions of pixels before they can get a reasonable enhancement that is valid and useable."

"Have they given you any idea whether they think they will be successful?"

"We're still waiting on an assessment of that, too." He rubbed his temples and glanced at her. "Now you know how frustrating this can be."

"No kidding! It sounds like agony. I don't think I would have the patience, George. You must be very anxious to find out whether the enhanced pictures will be useful."

"Absolutely. It would help our case immensely if we could identify the people on the images."

Marilee looked at him a long moment. George, being a detective, missed nothing. "What's going on, Marilee? Do you have something up your sleeve? You look like the cat who swallowed a canary."

Marilee laughed at the image it conjured in her mind. Thankfully, she had never seen a cat with a canary in its mouth. She would have been tempted to rescue the poor canary.

"There is an idea I want to mention to you. It's actually a partial idea, at this stage, but I thought that maybe we could figure out how to use it."

"Okay, shoot." His face was open, willing to hear whatever she had to say.

She was hesitant. She preferred ideas to be fully formed before she blurted them out. Damn! She would have to proceed without that comfort this time. She inhaled before spewing out the half-baked idea.

"Judging from the Platson murder and break-in at his house, the killer seems to be under the impression that the photos captured a clear image of him." She paused to ensure that George was following. He nodded. She continued.

"Since no one knows that the card has been found, the killer doesn't know it either. I think we should use this information to our advantage and set a trap to force the killer to reveal himself." As excited as she had been a moment ago, she now slumped, deflated, in her seat. "That's where I'm stuck. I don't know what type of trap we can set with this information. We have to give it some thought." She looked at him hopefully.

He leaned back in his chair and steepled his fingers under his chin. "In fact, I have been discussing just such a plan with Jim, and that is why I asked you to keep quiet about finding the card. And you still haven't said anything, right?"

"The only person I've mentioned it to is my mother and that was this morning. By the way, before I forget, I have to give credit where credit's due. It was my mother's idea."

"Smart lady. Is she in Florida or in town for a visit?" he asked conversationally. In the background, his mind was contemplating his next move.

"Yes, she's here for a visit. I'm glad she is, too. We always have such a great time, and I enjoy having someone around the house on occasion."

Half listening, he came to a decision; the time was right to set up and execute a trap. He picked up the receiver and dialed. Speaking quickly, he requesting Jim to join them in his office. On Jim's arrival, he closed the door, and the plan they had been plotting was laid out to Marilee in full detail.

"I want to let it be known that the card has been found." He looked at her seriously. "I am not proposing to put you at risk, Marilee. I'm suggesting that you tell everyone that you have found the card, and will keep it secured in your office until you can hand it over to the police. Do you have somewhere you can keep it?"

"Yes, we have a safe."

"Okay, so tell everyone that's where it is. Don't make it sound like you are trying to broadcast this information, otherwise the killer will see through our charade, but get the information out there. We have limited time to make this work."

"I think I can do that." She paused, and his last comment registered. "Are you expecting the killer to show up at the garden center tonight?"

"Hopefully."

"So you will have people there all night to keep a lookout for him and nab him if he shows up?"

"Exactly. The police will surround the premises and apprehend anyone who enters the premises tonight."

"Yikes! Will that be safe?"

George laughed, then resumed his serious demeanor. "I think we'll manage, Marilee. We have dealt with these types of situations before. Do you know how many businesses in this area are broken into every night?"

"I shudder to think about it."

"That's right. And because in this case we're dealing with a murderer, we will take extra precautions. Everyone wants this guy caught. So, Marilee, are you okay with everything we've discussed? You know your part?"

"Yes." She quickly reviewed her assigned activities. "So should I expect to see you after closing? Do you want me to stay behind to wait for you?"

"No, that would raise suspicions. We will coordinate everything by telephone. That reminds me, give me your cell phone number." They exchanged numbers.

"So just go home like normal today, Marilee. What are your hours again?"

"We close at 8 PM. Thankfully, the days are so long now that it's still light out at that time."

Jim made a note in his pad. "Perfect."

~

Her drive back to the shop was tense as she imagined how the evening would unfold. 2:30 PM was the time on her watch. She would have to keep it together until closing time, to give the impression that everything was normal, with the exception that she had found the memory card. How was she going to do that with credibility? A visit to the shrub lots was in order, to pretend to search for and find the missing card. Yes, that was probably the best approach. As she entered the parking lot, she took a deep breath. The charade was about to begin.

Yikes! The car jerked as she executed a sharp u-turn back out of the parking lot. That was close. She had almost forgotten that she would need a decoy memory card to effectively pull off the farce. A silent curse was directed at George. He could have at least warned her about that, or, even better, given her another card to use.

Twenty minutes later she pulled into the lot again, ready to carry out the artificial event. In preparation, she had already removed the card from its wrapping and secreted it in her pocket, to be retrieved at the right time, followed by the necessary hoopla and noise as she announced her discovery. She took several deep breaths as she hoped she could pull it off without anyone becoming suspicious, and stepped out of the car.

An hour later she was back in her office, closed the door and leaned against it, her heart beating. It was unnatural for her to act in such a duplicitous fashion, and she regretted lying to her staff, with whom she had always tried to be truthful and honest.

The desk chair beckoned her to rest her weary body and she slumped into it, exhausted, and rested her head on the desk on top of her crossed arms. Now she would just have to survive the rest of the day. Although the hard part seemed to be over, her staff and patrons having been given the information required to start the gossip chain through the community, she knew she would still face questions for the rest of the day. Too bad she couldn't stay in her office. Could she? She longed to hide from everyone, to avoid perpetuating the lie she had become so comfortable spreading in the last hour. Hopefully everything would be over by the morning. She propped one eye open to look at her watch and groaned. Only 3:45 PM!

As closing time neared, she became nervous and started biting her lip. What if she had failed to get the news to the killer? Sure, there had been a lot of comings and goings in the garden center. And her staff had hopefully done their part, chatting with the customers and others when they went off shift. She had never foreseen a day when she would be glad there was so much gossiping. Normally, she wanted her staff to focus on helping customers, not learning that Mrs. Jackson's cat had just given birth to six kittens. She brushed a hand across her brow to tame a stray strand of hair.

Her watch showed 7:20 PM when she started considering the night's events. How she wanted to be part of it! But that was foolish and surely George would say she was in the way. And in fact, although it seemed so long ago, it was actually still Mother's Day, and her plan had been to spend the evening with her mother. She sighed. She would have to wait it out at home.

Just after 8 PM she performed her normal lock-up routine, although, if anyone had been paying attention, they would have noticed that she was being extra cautious to ensure that no one was left on the premises. She would be very upset if her staff were caught in the crossfire, if things escalated to that. Once she had checked and double-checked everything, she returned to her office, closed the door and called George on his cellular phone.

"Everyone's gone, and I've locked up, George."

"Great. Where are you now?"

"I'm just heading out myself. I promised to spend the evening with my mother. You know, Mother's Day."

"Wish her well from me," he replied. "And Marilee, I know you're thinking it, but do not show up here at any time tonight, okay? I don't want anything to happen to you."

"Understood, George."

"Hopefully, this trap will work. For everyone's sake, I hope it does. Otherwise, we'll have to reassess our strategy tomorrow."

"Good luck and stay safe, George."

"Thanks, Marilee. If we need anything, we'll give you a call. And if we catch the killer, we'll let you know too. Bye."

"Bye." She returned the receiver softly to the cradle, and hoped that everything would unfold as planned. Retrieving her handbag from the back of the chair, she grabbed the car keys from the desk and made her way to the car.

It was now 8:23 PM, and dusk was starting to close in, creating eerie shadows as she moved quickly to her car. For some reason, she was now anxious to leave, uncomfortable with being the only person left on the premises.

~

George and Jim had been on the road just arriving at Marilee's garden center when she called from her office. Now, from their unmarked car camouflaged by the dense and neglected shrubbery opposite, they watched her back out of the spot and head towards the gate, where she got out to chain and lock the two large metal cross-beamed entrance barriers before jumping back into her car and heading off towards her home.

Jim called the other officers on their ear sets, checking that everyone was in position and invisible. Knowing it could turn out to be a long night, they had come equipped with everything they would need: coffee thermoses, sugary snacks and a couple of ham and cheese sandwiches. If it became necessary, everyone was prepared to take shifts napping while their partner kept watch.

Jim secretly hoped that the killer would show up sooner rather than later, so he could salvage a half-decent night's sleep. He envisioned his wife preparing the kids for bed, and regretted that he would not be there to tuck them in, and her too for that matter, he thought amorously.

George slapped him on the arm.

"What?" Jim came back to reality. Oh, yeah, he was here with George. Ugh. He made a face as he contrasted his thoughts with the reality of being on this stake-out with George.

"Your eyes were all glazed over. Snap out of it! It's going to be a long night." George snapped his fingers to make his point.

"Just thinking about where I'd rather be this evening," Jim replied ruefully.

George remained silent. He knew the feeling, but there was no helping it. Anyway, how often did they actually go on stake-outs? Infrequently, in a quiet community such as Sandalwood. He hoped it would stay that way. He raised the night-vision binoculars to his eyes to sweep the grounds, and found nothing unusual. Earlier in the day, unknown to Marilee, they had placed wireless microphones strategically on the property, specifically near the office, and other areas where they expected the killer to make his entrance and each of the officers on patrol were able to hear if any unusual noises sounded. So far, everything was silent. Too bad they couldn't play cards; it would distract their attention from their surveillance. God, this was going to be boring with a capital B!

Suddenly they heard muffled sounds coming from the office area of the garden center. It sounded like papers rustling and falling in a loud crinkle to the floor. Then, the sound of papers rustling again, as if someone was searching through them. Odd, thought George.

"Angus, go check it out. Be very quiet. If this is not our killer, I don't want to give away that we're here."

"Yes, sir," came the staticky reply from Angus.

Tense moments followed. They could hear the sound of Angus' stealthy movements as he entered the shop proper, treading carefully as he went. Other sounds accompanied his movements, emitted from other microphones. George and Jim looked at each other alertly, ready to bolt to Angus' defense.

"Sir," came a whispered message from Angus.

"Yes? What is it?"

"It's just the cat. Seems he was chasing a bird that got trapped in the office."

George and Jim gave a collective sigh of relief.

"Sir?"

"Yeah, get out of there right now."

"On my way."

George rubbed his throbbing forehead. He hoped it wasn't going to be like this all night; false alarms causing everyone's heart rate to shoot up, all senses tingling, ready for action. An aspirin, that's what he needed. He reached into his coat pocket and retrieved the little plastic bottle he carried with him at all times. It came in handy for moments like these, and he resorted to it often. Jim watched as he helped himself to a couple.

"Me too," said Jim as he stretched out his hand. George obligingly offered up the bottle for Jim to help himself to as many as he thought necessary.

The hours passed. The only message they had received since Angus' foray onto the premises was one when he returned to his surveillance partner.

~

At home, Marilee was trying to relax in the company of her mother. She had told her about the events planned for the evening, and now they were both anxious for a resolution without anyone getting hurt. *Except perhaps the murderer,* she thought vengefully. They decided to play the four-letter word game to occupy their minds until they received word from George or fell asleep waiting.

Each of them had chosen their secret four-letter word, and now the other was trying to guess it.

Stephanie started. "I guess 'once'". They both wrote it down.

"Hah," said her daughter. "Zero letters correct."

Stephanie was elated. That meant that her daughter's secret word did not contain any of the letters in the word 'once', which would help her narrow down the letters that her word *did* contain. She had eliminated two vowels.

Marilee gnawed at her fingernails. She was having a hard time concentrating.

"Bear."

"Zero." Again, they both wrote down the results. So far, they were even.

"Hair". Stephanie asked, trying to cover off more vowels.

"One."

"My turn." Marilee took a sip of her Australian Shiraz. "Oink."

Stephanie looked at her sideways. "Is that a real word?"

Marilee giggled. "I think so." She reached for the dictionary, a valuable tool for this game, not just for Scrabble. She flipped the worn pages of the Oxford Complete Wordfinder to 'O'. "Yup, it's in here." She said, pointing at a spot on the page.

Stephanie looked over her daughter's shoulder, checking that she wasn't cheating. "Okay, two."

An enthusiastic arm pumping came from Marilee. "Yes," she said, "I'll have your word figured out in no time."

"You wish," responded her mother, challenging her. "Okay, my turn. I guess 'spay'".

"Two." Marilee glanced nervously at her watch, hoping for news from George. It was almost 11:30 PM. What was happening at Green Horizons?

~

In the meantime, George, Jim, Angus and the rest of the surveillance team continued to watch Green Horizons. It was always the same during stake-outs: first you were all keyed up, adrenaline ready to pound through your system in preparation for action. Eventually, this developed into boredom, then annoyance, then a desire to sleep. Each stage reduced the attention of the observer, and the danger of missing something important grew. They had been trained to recognize these signs and remain on alert regardless of the signals their sedentary bodies sent them.

The night had grown dark. For the first time, George noticed the insufficiency of street lighting illuminating the premises. He made a mental note to tell Marilee that she should at least get some lighting on her place. Even some motion-detection lighting would be good. He chuckled to himself, envisioning the roaming raccoons that would most likely be the cause of most of the lights being tripped. So be it. It was better than the flip side of that coin.

He watched Jim snooze and envied him the chance to take a break from the surveillance. They had agreed that they would each take a couple of hours sleep, then switch.

Chapter 23

▼

The luminous dial of his watch showed 12:15 AM. It was time to check in with the other teams. He called each one in turn, requesting an update. "All clear" was the unanimous response. He sighed, realizing it was too late to call his wife. He doubted that she would appreciate him calling her to fill his minutes, considering she was probably already comfortably asleep. He knew of other spouses who were sleepless when their police officer husbands or wives were on a stake-out, and they managed to keep up an ongoing chat to while away the long hours. Usually that worked well when the surveillance was only visual. In this case, with the microphones, it would not be a workable distraction.

Cautiously he opened the car door. He needed some fresh air, and a chance to stretch his legs and back. Disturbed from his sleep, his surveillance partner stirred and turned his back to the open door, away from the cool night air. Surprisingly, the open field behind him was much louder than he had anticipated. The night air was filled with croaking frogs and rustling boughs of last year's dried grasses. A flock of Canada geese flew overhead, honking loudly to ensure they stayed together during their flight to who knew where. Probably some familiar overnight resting place. In the silence of the field, he could actually hear the whoop of their wings beating the still night air. He was surprised that they flew so late into the night, but perhaps nighttime flights were imperative to achieving the long distances they migrated every year.

A cool dampness was starting to creep into the night, and he felt the chill of it through his overcoat. Somewhere behind him he heard movement through the brush. He suspected that it was some nocturnal creature, foraging for prey in the vacant, wild field. Nonetheless, he turned quietly and focused his binoculars towards the origin of the sound to confirm his hunch. It certainly wouldn't do for him to succumb to his assumption, and find out the killer had crept up behind him. What would that say about his detecting skills? Not much, he thought ruefully. He would be the laughing stock of the department, even if he had been cracked over the head by the murderer in the process. No, his colleagues would have little sympathy for him. He'd be the butt of jokes until the next unfortunate person committed a gaff, taking the focus off him. He knew how that went.

As he trained his binoculars into the darkness, his sights landed on two does making their way almost silently through the tall weeds and dried grasses, while underfoot their hooves crunched on new growth.

A barn owl screeched nearby. He shivered at the feelings of isolation the noises created. This evening would be a lot nicer curled up in bed under the comforter with his wife, Vivian, than spending it out here in this eerie night, thought George, as he sighed wistfully.

~

They shouldn't have uncorked that bottle of wine. Marilee couldn't keep her eyes open, despite her anxiety about the goings-on at the garden center. She glanced at her mother, who was valiantly trying to keep up with her daughter.

"Mom," she said, shaking her gently. "Go to bed. We can finish this game tomorrow."

Her mother looked at her through half open eyes and placed her almost-empty glass carefully on the nearby coffee table.

"You're right. I think I've had it. Wake me if anything happens, will you?"

"Of course, Mom. You'll be the first to know." She leaned over and gave her mother a peck on the cheek. Another glance at her watch revealed that it was 1:45 AM. She hoped that everything was all right. Since she hadn't heard back from George, she assumed that nothing had happened. She started to worry. What if their efforts failed to pay off? Did George have any other ideas up his sleeve? Perhaps the photos would give up their secrets once the police had worked their magic on them. Something had to work. She prayed that tonight would be fruitful.

She rose unsteadily and carried the wine glasses to the kitchen to rinse them before heading to her cozy bed. As she slipped between the covers, she nudged Cinder out of the way to make room for her legs. The cat made a great hot water bottle, but he took up a surprising amount of space for such a small animal. *What a hog*, was the last thought she had as she fell into a deep, wine-induced slumber.

~

Jim watched the entrance to Marilee's garden center. 2:30 AM. So much for a good night's sleep, he thought, although he couldn't complain too much. George had taken an early watch, letting Jim have the first sleep, and he felt awake, despite the fact that it had only been a two-hour nap. Where was that damn intruder, he thought, frustrated by the wasted hours. Considering the business closed at eight o'clock, and it was fully dark by ten, the perpetrator could very well break into the place any time. Why did he have to wait for the middle, I mean middle, of the bloody night? If he was even planning to show up, he thought skeptically. What if he had seen through their ruse and was not planning to break into Marilee's safe tonight?

All sorts of negative thoughts intruded into his irritated mind. Perhaps they should have made it easier for him. How was he going to break into the safe anyway? Did he have skills as a safecracker? Was he planning on carting the safe away, to work on at his leisure? If so, he hoped that Marilee had emptied it of anything valuable. In fact, he hoped that she had done that anyway. How much did Marilee's safe weigh? Jim had not seen it, or he would have been able to hazard a good estimate.

A typical safe was two hundred and fifty pounds. Would the intruder have the physical strength to carry it away? Jim chuckled. Not without making one heck of a racket, that's for sure. He contemplated how he would go about carting away a fifty-pound safe, if he were so inclined. He was physically fit and worked out at the gym, two, sometimes three times a week. But a smaller, weaker person? What would they do? He imagined all sorts of creative approaches. You could wrap a thick rope or chain around it, drape the loose end over your shoulder and drag it. Now that would make one hell of a racket. Or you could try to tumble it out of the building, and use a plank to leverage it into the car. Hmm. That idea seemed fraught with flaws. While it seemed easy enough to remove it from the building, getting it into the car seemed problematic. How about this? Leaving the safe in place, you could blast a hole in it, and retrieve the contents. He snickered. He'd seen the aftermath of that before. He shook his head as he thought back to previous cases. Criminals, they thought they were so smart. They would lay their hands on some C4 explosives, and apply a thick wad of it on the door of the safe. Afraid it would be insufficient, and lacking enough C4 to make two attempts if a smaller amount proved unsuccessful, they usually blew the safe and all its contents to kingdom come, not to mention the physical injury they inflicted on themselves. Fortunately, it tended to work in the police's favor, because the thief was usually so frightened by the blast and his injuries that he would either call 911 or show up at the closest hospital looking for medical treatment. Hospital staff had enough experience to recognize the signs of a poorly executed crime, especially when the patient was unable to explain the reason for his burns, and invariably called police, who promptly carted the culprit off to jail once basic first aid had been applied.

Anyway, who was he kidding? If the killer showed up tonight, he and George would have to spend the rest of the night interrogating him and writing up reports. He sighed, realizing that the night was a write-off any way he looked at it. It was a good thing that he loved his detective job. The occasional overnight work was not that bad. It sure beat being a police officer on mind-numbing traffic duty.

He wondered who the murderer was. The police had a number of suspects under consideration, not the least of which were Glenda Platson and Stan's illegitimate son, Tom Dearling.

His bet was on the wife. *Let's face it,* he thought, *it's always the spouse. Yup, that's where he'd put his money.* He wondered whether she had manipulated Jack Talbot into committing the crime for her, or whether she had had the nerve to carry it out herself. He listed the facts that pointed to her: One, she knew where he was. Two, she had been to Green Horizons before, and knew the layout. Three, if Stanford had mentioned his purchasing plans to her, she knew exactly what aisle he would be in, and could plant (no pun intended) herself nearby and kill him in a matter of seconds. He paused. What else was there? Oh yes, and there was the matter of the insurance money. So, four, a substantial life insurance policy. He could go on forever: Five, she seemed to have an active social life and Stanford seemed to be drag on it. Six, maybe she had been carrying on an affair with Jack for some time, and they had decided they wanted to be together all the time, and that Stanford was a huge hindrance to their future happiness.

Yes, it was a substantial list. He wondered: if Jack had not swung the murder weapon for her, was she physically capable of doing it? He contemplated for a moment, weighing the factors. The murder weapon was light. How had she known a garden tool would be accessible? Or did she come prepared with a different plan, came across the cultivator and decided to use it, instead? It was possible. But that the first swing had achieved her goal, there had to be an element of luck in that, he mused. The claws had entered his body in such a way as to glance off the ribs and sink right between them and into the heart.

He rubbed his chest, visualizing the moment of impact and shuddered, remembering his visit to the morgue where he had attended a segment of Stanford's autopsy. It had been, let's see, five years since he had attended his first one, and still he was uncomfortable. He tried his best to wrangle out of them, but his boss insisted he attend. He said it provided so much more information than reading the tidy, clinical autopsy report later. His boss was probably right, but his stomach revolted every time he found out he would have to witness one, and he often lost his breakfast or lunch over it. He'd seen worse than Stanford's though. He thought back to a case where they had fished a thirty-year-old cottager from a lake after he had been under water for five months. Ugh. Now that, that was gross.

He refocused his mind to remove the morbid images from his thoughts. Okay, Tom Dearling. Not his favorite suspect, but a suspect nonetheless. Certainly George and he had thought there was a possibility that Tom had committed the crime when they had escorted him to the police station the other day. Personally, Jim thought the case was weak, but could see that there were some factors that made him an attractive suspect. He started numbering again. One, he was related to the victim. Two, the victim presumably was ignorant of the fact that Tom was his illegitimate son, and perhaps either Tom or Diedre had confronted Stan and demanded money. He scratched his chin, feeling the stubble that had grown since the morning. He checked his watch. Yikes, only ten minutes since he had last checked. God, the hands were moving slowly tonight. He evaluated his list. Hmm. Was there more to add? Oh yes, he had opportunity: Tom worked where Stan was killed. Now that *was* suspicious. On the other hand, he was pretty scrawny, and Jim doubted he'd have the manual force to deliver the fatal blow.

Suddenly, subtle noises emanated from the speaker. He focused his hearing acutely on the indistinct sounds. Yes, there they were again. Slight scraping sounds. He wondered what it was. Someone trying to jimmy the lock to get into the office? Perhaps. A metallic click carried over the small speaker, and Jim's heightened senses told him he had been right.

He nudged George in the ribs with his elbow, and held his index finger to his lips, while pointing at the speaker with his other hand. George, instantly alert, followed Jim's direction.

The remote sounds became more pronounced. Apparently the intruder assumed (wrongfully) he was alone, and safe to make noise inside the garden center at, what time was it? 2:45 AM.

Soon it would be time to make their move, but not yet. They wanted further confirmation that he (she?) was inside the premises, and, preferably, with the goods in his hands, so they could catch him red-handed. It would hardly do to storm the place and find out they'd been spurred into action by that blasted orange cat.

George whispered urgently into the microphone. "Everyone, I hope you heard that. We have activity on the premises. Be ready to take action. I'll let you know when."

A series of 'yes, sir' came from the teams. Good, that meant they were all awake, alert and ready.

More footsteps. Jim wondered whether Marilee had left her office door open or shut. It would have been better to ask her to close the door, so they could hear the intruder open it. No problem. And in fact, depending on how familiar the intruder was with the building (he was thinking of Tom), it might warn him off if he found Marilee's normally open office door closed.

The intruder must have felt greater confidence, because now they could see the unsteady, yellow light of a flashlight moving through the vacant office. Okay, that was no cat! George spoke distinctly into the microphone, ordering the teams to work their way slowly and quietly towards the light.

As if by agreement, although they hadn't spoken a word, he and Jim simultaneously stepped out of the car and quietly traversed the asphalt of the abandoned street. They both wore dark suits, typical attire for a stake-out, and headed silently towards the main entrance, where they paused, gave each other a signal that they were ready, and unholstered their revolvers.

Silently they slipped through the opening left by the trespasser and spread apart again, each taking one side of the open office area.

Once the other teams had assembled around the circumference of the office, George nodded his go-ahead to Angus and his partner. They made their way stealthily towards Marilee's office, where a beam of light threw shadows through the open doorway.

The lights in the office area were snapped on, and Angus shouted "Drop your weapon!" before charging at the intruder and wrestling him to the floor.

George and Jim entered behind him. Lying face down on the floor was a darkly clad figure, flashlight still in one hand, no weapon in sight. He writhed and struggled to free himself, to no avail.

"Don't bother squirming. This place is surrounded. You can't escape," said George firmly. "Jim, put some cuffs on this guy."

Jim obliged immediately and turned the intruder over, curious to identify the person who had been the subject of so many late nights and dead-end inquiries over the past weeks. While some of the officers were ignorant of the identity of the culprit, George recognized him.

It was Bill Trimly. He let out a deep breath, satisfied that they had achieved their objective and confident that they had caught the killer of Stanford Platson.

~

At 3:30 AM George placed a call to Marilee's home. Marilee answered groggily.

"Marilee, we caught him. I've posted officers around your property to keep it safe until you get here in the morning to check it all over and replace any broken locks and windows."

Marilee took a few minutes to digest it. "That's good. Who is it?"

"Bill Trimly."

Marilee tried to register the name. It sounded vaguely familiar but didn't ring any bells in her disoriented state. She tried to focus on the red illuminated digits on her nightstand. No wonder, she thought, reading the fuzzy numbers. It's the middle of the night.

"Thanks, George. I'll call you later," She hardly acknowledged her relief, although her brain registered it. Her eyes closed before her outstretched hand had even replaced the handset. The response seemed so inadequate, but George seemed to sense her appreciation, so he did not dwell on it. Tomorrow, when she had her senses about her, she would express her thanks to the team for having solved the crime and rid the community of a dangerous killer.

~

In the morning Marilee woke with a start, vaguely remembering George's call from earlier that morning. *My God, I've got to get down there,* she thought immediately. She padded softly to her mother's room to give her the good news, showered and dressed. Who had George said they had captured? She racked her brain for the name. It wasn't one she had expected. Bill Trimly, that was it. Who the heck is that? She mulled it over thoughtfully while she ate a hasty breakfast of cold cereal and milk.

Popping her head into her mother's room she said a quick good-bye, and wished her a great day, promising to be home early to take her to the airport for her return to Florida. What a quick visit that was, she thought, thinking that it had seemed a lot faster than usual because of all the goings-on.

A short drive later she was at work. Pete had already arrived, and was wondering why uniformed police officers were guarding the place. In a brief conversation Marilee explained that there had been a break-in. The more detailed version would have to wait until later.

A bedraggled George met her. After greeting him and the officers, he asked her to check for damage and missing items. Everything seemed fine. It appears that the intruder had jimmied the lock on the door, causing no permanent damage. Her office seemed a bit of a mess, like a tornado had struck it, but what did you expect with a midnight arrest by who knows how many officers in a space no bigger than ten foot by ten foot? Nothing looked to be missing, although the two hundred and fifty-pound safe seemed to have been moved, but not opened.

"Please open the safe to ensure that nothing has been taken. We searched Bill thoroughly this morning, but I would like to be sure."

He handed her a translucent pair of white, latex gloves and Marilee complied. Yes, the decoy and a handful of meaningless papers remained in the safe, just as she'd left them yesterday.

"Marilee, we're going to need a written statement from you. I'm heading back to the station now. Would you be able to follow me, so we can get this taken care of?"

"Absolutely," nodded Marilee, wanting to be as helpful as possible. No doubt an overtired George was a cranky George. "I'll just have a word with Pete and Jane."

"Great, thanks, Marilee. I'll see you at the station in, let's say, half an hour?"

"Yup. No problem." George headed out the door. She hoped for his sake that he would be able to call it an early day, and take a much-deserved rest.

~

Before she had a chance to seek out Pete and Jane, her mind flew back to the murderer's name. Bill Trimly. The name still did not shake anything lose in her mind. For some reason, only Sarah's name emerged. Sarah? She would have to call her. Yes, perhaps somehow,

Sarah was the key to this. A few minutes later, she had her answer. After a momentary pause, Sarah had zeroed in on it.

"Remember when you asked me to check the building permit records?" She was whispering, and rightly so. She was at work.

"Yes. And you didn't find any discrepancies or evidence of wrongdoing."

"Right. But he was one of the three building inspectors I mentioned to you. I can't remember the other two at the moment, but give me some time and I'll try to remember their names. Anyway, he did a number of building inspections on Charles Kingly's roofing installations, remember?"

Marilee remembered, all right. She quickly thanked Sarah and hung up. Okay, so how did this tie? She was getting confused. Of all the people to have been caught in this trap, she hadn't expected it to be Bill Trimly, whom she even didn't know, and wouldn't recognize if she fell over him. Tom Dearling, yes. Glenda Platson, sure. Even Diedre Dearling. But Bill Trimly?

After providing Pete and Jane with brief instructions, she climbed into her FJ and made her way to the police station. It was still early in the morning, and there was little traffic on the roads, robbing her of the time she needed to put her thoughts together before pulling into the parking lot. Instead, once she arrived, she sat in the car, mulling the name over in her mind. The sun beat down on the roof of her car and she realized how hot the closed compartment had become. Distracted, she lowered the front driver's and passenger's side windows to permit some fresh air flow. Bill Trimly, Bill Trimly. Building inspections. Stanford Platson. Sturdy Roofing Installations. Stanford Platson. Financial controller. Charles Kingly. Stanford Platson. Stanford Platson. Stanford Platson. Bill Trimly.

An idea formed in her mind. It was the same thought she had had right after Stanford had been murdered. Was it possible that, as a function of his role at Sturdy Roofing Installations, he had uncovered that Charles was bribing building inspectors? She became excited. Yes, the parts of the puzzle were rapidly falling into place. As the financial controller for Sturdy Roofing Installations, Stanford Platson was in charge of the financial records of the company, so he was aware of all payments the company made, all the flows of incoming and outgoing expenses. The expense incurred for the bribes would have to be entered in the books, but in order to hide their real purpose, they would have to be entered as some other expense, which required the complicity of the financial controller. Charles had brazenly assumed that he could rely on Stanford to go along with the scheme when he promoted him to financial controller. That had been a mistake. Once Stanford found odd entries in the books, he surmised that Charles was bribing the building inspectors, Bill Trimly at least, to approve his roofs without inspecting them, so that he could cut corners on materials and labor costs. Charles realized that Stanford was not prepared to play ball, and either he or Bill Trimly, his co-conspirator in the faulty permit scam, killed him.

That had to be it. It fit perfectly. She thought back to all of the events and conversations she had overheard. Charles Kingly speaking privately with someone in the coatroom about building inspections, and her conversation with Holly about the conversation she had overhead between Kingly and Platson. Marilee could bet that the two of them thought they were the only ones in the office when they had their blowup. Platson had confronted Kingly with the bribery, and told him that it had to stop, or something to that effect. And Kingly, being the arrogant and explosive man that he was, counter attacked with accusations of embezzlement to force Stanford's compliance. And it would have been an effective threat. With such a complaint against him, he would never work again. It also explained Stanford looking for a new job as he tried to save his reputation by changing employers before things boiled over between him and Charles. Yes! Marilee had it all figured out. She thumped the steering wheel in triumph. It was time to see George.

When George picked her up in the lobby, she noticed again how tired he looked. The entire case must have been a great drain on him. She felt very much like he looked, although she was surprisingly alert and insightful for having had such an interrupted night's sleep.

Making small talk, they headed to his office, where Jim was already comfortably seated. They reviewed the morning's events and updated each other to fill in the missing pieces. Marilee was curious about Bill Trimly.

"So how is he?"

"Resting comfortably in his new cell." Jim said sarcastically. The image of an irate Trimly manacled to the metal bed frame, where they had last seen him, filled him with satisfaction.

"I'll bet. Sounds like he should try to get used to it."

"Yes, I think so."

"Have you tried to find out anything from him yet?" She was curious to see whether Trimly had spilled the beans, and her theory was correct.

"Yes, we've been at it since we finished booking him. You know, photos, fingerprints and other documentation." Jim ran a tired hand over his scalp, creating spikes of disheveled hair.

"Has he said anything?"

"No, but he will." George said grimly slamming his fist on the desk. "So far, he's only glared at us, and swears he won't say a word without his lawyer being present. He just paces the room like a caged animal. It certainly does not give the impression he's in any way innocent of these crimes. Don't worry, we'll break him eventually." He seemed determined and his jaw muscles showed through his cheeks as he clamped his teeth in frustration.

"I'm sure he will eventually tell you the whole story. Has anyone figured out his connection to Stanford, and his motive?" She inquired curiously. There was no point outlining her theory if they had already stumbled on a better one, not that she could imagine a better theory than hers.

"Not yet. It is unclear what his connection is to Platson. We called his wife this morning, but she had never heard the name until we mentioned it to her today. But that may not be so unusual. People's spouses don't always know the same people they do, especially work-related ones."

Marilee's certainty about the potential motive grew. She was positive that Platson had been killed because he had captured images of Bill Trimly accepting bribes from Charles Kingly. She took a deep breath, preparing herself for possible ridicule, not that she really expected it. But you never knew.

George and Jim's eyebrows rose with incredulity as she laid out her theory for the crimes.

"We should be thankful that no buildings have collapsed," she continued. "Can you imagine? Sturdy installed roofs for all types of industrial and commercial buildings, as well as hospitals and schools. What if a school roof had collapsed? He tendered on the St. Michael's Grade School roof three years ago, and the school went into use last year. It is horrific to imagine that roof collapsing during school hours, with all of the students and faculty in attendance. I wonder how long the bribery has been going on. This could go back many years and many buildings." She shook her head in dismay. That anyone could even consider risking the people's lives for personal financial gain was beyond her. The sad part was that it probably happened more often than she thought. She sighed.

In the meantime, George and Jim were totally flabbergasted as they struggled to catch up to her. Once the interlocking parts of her theory had sunk in, George's brow furrowed. He looked seriously at Jim. They could not believe they had had no idea about the far-reaching effects of the crime until now. Marilee could tell George was fuming. Not at the situation, but at Charles' and Bill's short-sightedness and selfishness. It was beyond comprehension.

"Jim, you and I are going to start some intensive interrogation with Bill the minute we're done here. If what Marilee says is true, it has far-reaching implications. We will have to determine how wide spread this is, and have the questionable buildings re-inspected."

Marilee heaved a heavy sigh of relief. It was over.

Epilogue

Sandalwood gradually returned to normal. Its residents went back to their usual routines, relief written on the faces of pedestrians and in passing cars. Of course, the Sandalwood Chronicle was the first to publish the news, and was delighted by the increased circulation the semi-weekly publication achieved through the horrific story.

After intensive interrogation, Bill Trimly had broken down and provided a detailed recounting of his illegal dealings with Sturdy Roofing Installations, and how it had lead to the murder of Stanford Platson, which he vehemently denied committing, preferring to lay the blame on Charles Kingly. No one was fooled, as his partial fingerprints had been collected from the murder weapon. Charles Kingly was later arrested at his home on charges of bribery and complicity to murder as well as to numerous building code offences. In addition to his murder and bribery charges, Trimly was later charged with breaking and entering, his DNA and fingerprints having been found in the Platson household. Both faced long stretches in prison. Not only did they turn out to be stupid, but also careless, criminals. Hadn't they heard of latex gloves?

How Kingly had convinced Trimly to take care of the 'dirty work' was beyond comprehension. Kingly hadn't been at either scene, based on the evidence. Either it was a sly move on his part, or perhaps his physical size (he was a large, heavy man) had precluded his direct involvement, making Trimly the clear choice to commit both the murder and break-in. Marilee hoped it would not diminish the case against Kingly. In her estimation he was neck deep in every aspect of these crimes. Envisioning Kingly's possible next move, she could foresee his pleading ignorance of the murder. She hoped the courts would not accept this implausible and unlikely defense.

The need for the ambush that resulted in the criminals' arrest proved itself when the police department's forensic department was unable to further enhance the images to permit identification of the criminals.

Later, the municipal building permit department was fully investigated to determine the extent of the corruption. In the end, it was determined that only Bill Trimly had been involved, and the community sighed a collective breath, knowing that the majority of area buildings were considered unaffected by the findings. A list of potentially unsafe buildings was published in the Chronicle and national papers, and business and institutions were temporarily housed in alternative premises at great expense until rigorous inspections could be completed. A school in neighboring Meadowfield, which had recently succumbed to fire, was later found to be one of the buildings Sturdy Building Installations had roofed.

Tom Dearling and his mother moved away from Sandalwood. It seemed she had found a better job in a neighboring state as a veterinarian's receptionist. A friend of Diedre's, a co-worker at the Buy and Save, later confided to Marilee that at the age of twenty Diedre had carried on an brief affair with, unknown to her, a married man, namely Stanford Platson. When he found out she was pregnant, he abandoned her.

The story explained a lot. Marilee wondered when Stanford had become aware that Diedre and Tom had moved to Sandalwood. She surmised that he must have been petrified that his past indiscretions would be revealed. It would have been interesting to know whether either of them ever did approach him to ask him to recognize his illegitimate son. If so, his failure to respond positively was surely a sign that he was afraid his wife would react badly and leave him. What other reason could there be? She wondered if that was true, or had Stanford underestimated his wife's love, understanding and compassion? Marilee would never know the answer to that question, but this much was certain: what, in life, could be greater fulfillment than to create, acknowledge and raise a human being in your own image? Perhaps he felt fulfilled by the two legitimate children he had produced and reared to adulthood. She supposed she could ask Diedre or Tom if they had approached Stanford, but she hadn't the heart. What good would come of it? If they even gave her an honest answer, she thought skeptically. She could imagine that there would be no point now for them to admit such a conversation had ever taken place.

In contrast, Marilee found it interesting that Stanford had shown such fortitude in refusing to be drawn into the Kingly/Trimly fraud scheme. Perhaps he felt that a personal indiscretion was one thing, but a wholesale scam to put hundreds of lives at risk was not something he could live with. Or perhaps his early personal failings had created in him a desire to avoid future moral degradation, shoring his determination to stand firm in the face of pressure from his boss, Charles Kingly, to comply. In a way, Stanford had demonstrated admirable strength by not becoming involved in such an immoral and potentially lethal crime. Another thought crossed her mind. Had he seen the Meadowfield newspaper article and realized that the shortcomings of the scam were already playing themselves out? And, while he may not have had the nerve to turn Kingly and Trimly in to police, he at least had the decency and common sense not to become enmeshed with what was clearly a misguided scheme, by seeking employment elsewhere. For that, Glenda and Tom could be proud of him.

Marilee was pleased to hear that Tom was continuing his studies and was well on his way to becoming a qualified accountant. Sometimes, when she was prepared to admit it, she regretted having pointed her finger at Tom as his father's killer. How sad that things had turned out the way they did.

Later that year, to her surprise, Marilee was invited to the wedding of Glenda Platson and Jack Talbot. It took place at the botanical gardens, a fitting tribute, Marilee thought, to Stanford. She wondered if Glenda had made the connection. She thought not. For their honeymoon, she and Jack had plans to travel to the rainforests of Costa Rica to bring educational supplies to the area and help local children learn to read and write. On their return, they would settle in Georgia near Glenda's daughter and Jack's family. It was a far cry from her life just a few weeks ago. Marilee marveled at the change in her and, in her mind, congratulated her on coming through the changes so positively. She was like a phoenix risen from the ashes.

At the reception, Glenda Talbot glowed in a beautiful pale yellow gown embroidered with beads and sequins as she twirled around the dance floor on Jack's arm. Marilee caught her eye and raised her glass in a toast. Glenda's eyes twinkled back at her.

Later, Marilee drank champagne and chatted with the guests. In the background some of the traditional wedding activities were taking place. Marilee had no interest in watching Jack remove a garter from his new bride. A mass of yellow and white flew through her field of vision and landed in the crook of her arm. She looked down to find the wedding bouquet. She looked around her, bewildered, as everyone laughed and congratulated her on her luck. Oh no, she thought, not me!

About the Author

A.W. Zanetti lives in Ontario, Canada and earned a degree in Languages from the University of Toronto. A life-long lover of all things botanical, A.W. has surrounded the house with beautiful gardens and ponds, filling every available space with colorful plants. A.W. delights in observing a steady stream of winged visitors to the garden, its bordering stream and meadows.